How to SLAY a WEREWOLF

Written by Martin Howard
Illustrated by Sholto Walker

Ticktock

An Hachette UK Company
www.hachette.co.uk

First published in the USA in 2014 by Ticktock,
an imprint of Octopus Publishing Group Ltd
Endeavour House
189 Shaftesbury Avenue
London
WC2H 8JY
www.octopusbooks.co.uk
www.octopusbooksusa.com
www.ticktockbooks.com

Distributed in the US by
Hachette Book Group USA
237 Park Avenue
New York, NY 10017, USA

Distributed in Canada by
Canadian Manda Group
664 Annette Street
Toronto, Ontario, Canada M6S 2C8

ISBN 978 1 78325 113 1

Printed and bound in China

1 3 5 7 9 10 8 6 4 2

Project Editor: Catherine Coe Designer: Hannah Mee
Publisher: Samantha Sweeney Managing Editor: Karen Rigden
Production Controller: Sarah-Jayne Johnson US Editor: Jennifer Dixon

Contents

Professor
Van Helsing Phd BA Dip GNVQ
BSC PGCE
HND

Chapter 1

Welcome, Young Slayer

They call me mad. **MAD!** Me, the great Professor Van Helsing, who has saved the world from Evil more times than you have picked your nose. Me, who has done battle with demons while armed only with a ball of string and my genius! Me, who invented the **Exploding Chicken.**[1]

I am not mad (except on Thursday afternoons). It is all true. All of it! Evil walks and crawls and slithers among us. In the darkness there are teeth, claws, and disgusting, drooling things with red, boggly eyes. The monsters never stop coming, and someone must put up a fight. Admittedly, I am now old. My hair is white and difficult to control. My ears are shriveled. My knees are creaky and freckled. Once, I could chase a werewolf through the darkness all night long, but now I sometimes cannot reach the bathroom in time. Even so, I still have my gadgets and a lifetime of experience. Rickety and elderly I may be, but the werewolf that tangles with Van Helsing is a werewolf that's going to wish it had stayed at home, licking its own behind. Disgusting, **filthy creatures.**

[1] Guaranteed to kill all known werewolves – only $19.99 from the Van Helsing Slayer Supplies and Equipment Company. Free delivery with orders over $50.

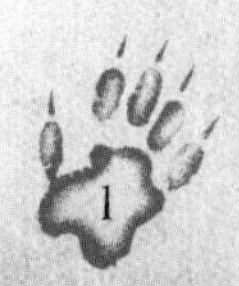

DUMMKOPF
SCIENTIA
THE MAJESTIC LORD HIGH WIZARD
of the great
UNIVERSITY OF DUMMKOPF
(which is a respectable university no matter what anyone says)
declares that
Ulrich Viktor Van Helsing
has passed some exam or other.
Possibly. The papers got a bit mixed up. Still, well done him!
He is hereby awarded the title of
PROFESSOR OF DEMONOLOGICAL RESEARCH
and is now qualified to slay
Creatures of Evil wherever he may find them.
SIGNED
HIS GRANDNESS, THE MAJESTIC LORD HIGH WIZARD
UNIVERSITY OF DUMMKOPF (A RESPECTABLE UNIVERSITY)

In these pages, dear reader, I will impart all of my memories, my **knowledge**, and my experience, so that you, too, can become a slayer. Join me. Not only will you be helping to **rid** the world of the diabolical forces of **Evil**, but it's jolly good fun, too. There are people who think that a slayer must be some kind of Chosen One, with **special powers** or **magical weapons**. They are wrong. With this book, anyone can be a slayer. Just you wait and see. It is difficult to believe, but even I, the great Van Helsing, was once just an ordinary boy.

"Ha ha," I hear you say, "the legendary Van Helsing - ordinary? It is not possible."

But Van Helsing never lies.

How I Came to Be a Slayer

My story began many years ago, in the small German town of **Grüselighausen**. Oh, the fun I had wading through the swamps, exploring the ruined castles, and getting lost in the forests! But that was before **Great-Aunt Hellga** showed me that the world is infested with Evil.

She was a quiet woman, **Great-Aunt Hellga** - the sort of great-aunt who knits socks and wears a frilly cap. She was a little hairy, it's true, but great-aunts so often *are* hairy, aren't they? I remember she was always sucking a mint. Her breath smelled so bad it made you want to pull your own nose off.

I thought nothing of this until a creaking floorboard woke me late one night. By the light of the full moon pouring through my bedroom window, I saw a beast creep into my room - a beast that looked like **Great-Aunt Hellga!**

My great-aunt was even hairier than usual – her head, neck, and arms were covered in black **fur** – and she was walking on all fours. Her face had... well, the thought of her face still gives me nightmares. Her great mouth was open and **dripping drool** upon the rug. Her teeth were **sharp** and shining in the moonlight. Her snout snuffled as she padded across the floor towards the cage that held my pet hamster. I was **terrified**.

Hardly daring to **breathe**, I did not move or make a sound as she reached into the cage with her horrid claws and grabbed poor, squeaking little **Freddï**.

As I watched her gobble him down in one bite, I knew I would spend the rest of my life **exterminating** monsters like Great-Aunt Hellga. For Freddï.

Poor **Freddï**. I still miss him.

It was a month until the next full moon.

In that time, I took my first steps on a path that would lead me to become the world-famous slayer that I am today. I asked

questions: why did the people of Grüselighausen lock themselves inside every night? If no one lived in any of the ruined castles, why could I see lights in their windows from my bedroom? Why did such a small town have so many **graveyards**, and why did so many of the graves have mailboxes?

Slowly, I uncovered the whispered truth: **Grüselighausen** was not only home to the living but to the ghastly undead, too. The town was **crawling** with Creatures of the Dark. Such as werewolves. Oh, there were lots and lots of werewolves. **Great-Aunt Hellga** was one of them.

There was one question at the front of my mind:
How do you slay a werewolf?

The answer to that **question**, and more, will be **revealed** within these pages. For now, let me just say that when the full moon rose again, **Great-Aunt Hellga** *mysteriously* vanished. A week later, I had a new werewolf-fur hat for the winter. Soon, rumors spread around Grüselighausen. As you can see from this small selection of the many letters I received, I soon became very **busy**...

Dear Young Master Van Helsing,

They say that you can be trusted.
Please help us! Granny's always been hairy but now my wife and I are having to shave her every day, and when we take her out shopping, she pees up against lampposts in the street.
The doctor says this is unusual in a woman of her age (granny is ninety-four).
Could she be a werewolf?
If so, my wife and I would be ever so grateful if you could come and slay her when you have a spare moment.

Yours sincerely,
Otto Böring

To the Van Helsing boy,

My husband is a horrible, badly trained beast who drools on the carpet and keeps scratching at the door to be let out at night. Please come and put him out of my misery.

Yours,

Grunhilde von Luftwigg

Greetings, young Van Helsing,

All of Grüselighausen is talking of your exploits. They say that you have come to deliver us from the werewolf curse! I would like to shake you by the hand, young man! In the meantime, I thought you might like to know that Horst Dagwurst at 83 Grossbotti Street has a very large beard. Also, he borrowed my lawnmower last week and has not returned it. Surely, the mark of a beast!

Sincerely,

Fritz Bludwurst
82 Grossbotti Street

PS: When you have slain Horst Dagwurst, please return the lawnmower to the shed at the back of my garden.

Van Helsing,

AAAAAARGGGHHH!!!!!

IT'S COMING IN THROUGH THE WINDOW.

LOOK AT THE SIZE OF ITS TEETH!

IT'S GOT MY FOOT!!!

HELP! HELP!!!!

Hoping this finds you and your family in excellent health.
I look forward to seeing you at your earliest convenience.

Yours sincerely,
Jürgen Niedöderliebenmunchkin-Lampschade.

Alone, I slayed them all. As the years passed, my fame spread. I traveled the world, always seeking out the **monsters** and inventing new and better ways to slay them, such as the *Van Helsing False-Bottom Concrete Fang-Breaker™*.

The Da

"FULL MOON" MURDERS OVER

"MAD" VAN HELSING CLAIMS WEREWOLF SLAIN

POLICE IN THE VILLAGE OF Bishopspiddle have released a statement saying the ghastly murders that shocked the country have stopped. "It's a mystery," said Chief Detective Roger Copper, scratching his head. "We were getting a ghastly murder every night during every full moon until that strange Van Helsing chap showed up. Then they stopped. Just like that. It wasn't anything to do with the police. We were just bumbling about in the dark without a clue. As usual."

The looney Professor Van Helsing, or "Mad Van" as he is usually known, told our reporter Jennifer Kidney, "It was a werewolf. I am NOT mad! Stop writing down that I am mad! I can see you doing it!"

He added, "Once again, the incredible and invincible Van Helsing has saved the day. Would you like to buy a fur coat? Genuine wolf. Reasonably priced."

In the light of day, the newspapers called me mad, but when night fell and the moon rose and the **wolves** began howling at the door, people always begged Professor Van Helsing to come.

...y Howl

FRIDAY, OCTOBER 13

"I am NOT mad," said the professor at Bishopspiddle yesterday.

YOUR TURN TO SLAY

Now, it's *your* turn. **Are you ready?**

Do not be afraid, for with the great **Van Helsing** guiding you, you'll soon be wearing your very own werewolf-fur hat. You must only be brave enough to stare hideous screaming horror in the face and poke it in the eye. Step by step, I will teach you everything you need to know about these fearsome creatures, including spotting a werewolf problem (the blood and **mangled** bodies usually give it away), how to **track** down your **prey**, and how to slay it with the minimum amount of fuss and bother. **Slaying** werewolves has never been so easy!

By the time you've finished this book, you'll be exterminating werewolves with absolute confidence. Only **Professor Van Helsing's** amazing advice can make this promise, so do not be fooled by impostors and imitators (especially Doctor Harold Von Dirtfinger's *Werewolf Slaying: A Beginner's Guide*, which is **hogwash**).

Happy slaying,

Don't get lost, get the Van Helsing

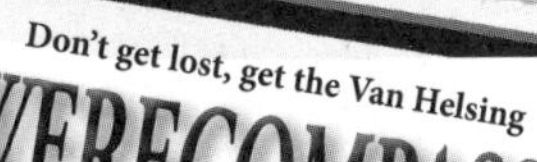

Using the latest magical technology, this handy gadget is powered by a drop of genuine werewolf blood. and always points to your prey.

No more wandering around desolate moors shouting, "Here, boy!"

Only $12.99

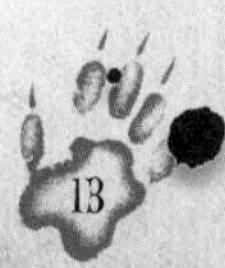

Chapter 2

Into the Jaws of Death

Ha, **young** slayer, I bet you want to get started. Probably already **sharpening** your weapons and thinking you might skip this chapter so you can read the grisly bits, eh? But no – put down that **crossbow** and stop stuffing that chicken with dynamite. You have just started on your journey. Soon, I will teach you how to slay, but first you must learn the truth about **werewolves**.

"But a werewolf is a werewolf is a werewolf," I hear you say. "Big chomping teeth, fur, etc. Stop babbling on, Van."

Wait.

As I always say: an unprepared **slayer** is a *dead* slayer. So **dead** they'll be able to fit what's left of you in a small paper bag. The werewolf, or ***Luposapian horribilis*** as we professors call it, is a fearsome beast. Once you see just how fearsome, you may decide to take up knitting instead.

Read on, if you **dare**...

What Is a Werewolf?

The word *werewolf* means "**man-wolf.**"[2] Some people think this means that the werewolf is just a **normal**, everyday wolf wearing ripped pants. If this were true, slaying them would be no problem. An old lady could do it with her handbag. In case you're wondering, **werewolves** are also not just normal humans who need flea shampoo, a visit to the dentist, and some nail clippers.[3]

In fact, the transformation from human to werewolf is **highly complex.** The werewolf is a mix of different parts of both wolf and human. From the wolf, the werewolf has intelligence, ferocity, speed, stealth, excellent hunting skills, and ultrasharp senses.

[2] The la-di-da scientific word for people who turn from human to wolf is "lycanthrope," but as it's rather a mouthful, even most scientists can't be bothered with it.

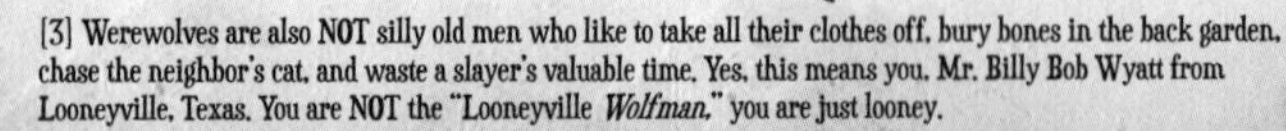

[3] Werewolves are also NOT silly old men who like to take all their clothes off, bury bones in the back garden, chase the neighbor's cat, and waste a slayer's valuable time. Yes, this means you, Mr. Billy Bob Wyatt from Looneyville, Texas. You are NOT the "Looneyville *Wolfman*," you are just looney.

From humans it has... ummm... the ability to look like a human (except during the **full moon**) and... errr... that's about it really.

But there is **more**.

Werewolves have strength and **healing powers** far beyond any real wolf or human, as well as an unquenchable thirst for terror and blood and – strangely – chickens. In fact, the werewolf is to a wolf what a great white shark is to a goldfish: they both look like fish but I know which one I would prefer to fight with my bare hands. In the same way, the werewolf might *look* like a huge, mad wolf with burning eyes and great **dripping jaws**, but it is *much*, much worse.

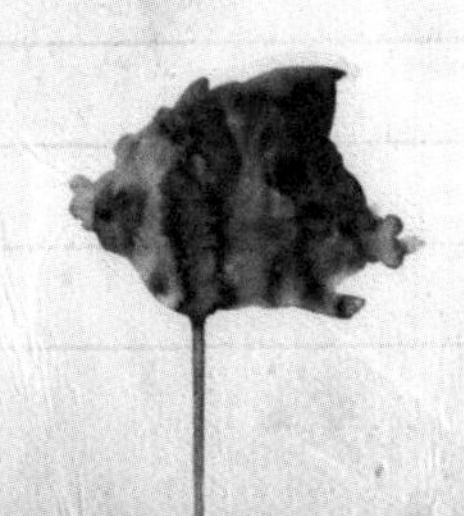

Myth Versus Reality

There are some things that many people get wrong about werewolves, but the slayer must know the truth...

MYTH 1:

Werewolves Aren't Real

WRONG. Most people go around laughing and jeering and pointing at anyone who thinks **werewolves** really exist. They even call them **"mad"**! Then they act surprised when they are eaten by one. Werewolves are as real as you and I. Of course, governments keep this information quiet. If the truth were known, everyone would run around screaming and waving their arms in the air. Here are just two of the Top-Secret files I have ~~stolen~~ collected, which prove their existence...

CLASSIFIED DOCUMENT LEVEL: ALPHA 1

ALERT LEVEL: RED

F.B.W.

Federal Bureau of Weirdness

TO: Professor Van Helsing

FROM: Harold J. Appliance (Director)

The prime minister of Britain has turned werewolf. Again. French ambassador eaten. Travel immediately to London. Fake passport and tickets enclosed. Take all necessary action to remove threat. Speak to no one. Usual payment.

FOR YOUR EYES ONLY.
DESTROY AFTER READING.

Harold J. Appliance

P.E.S.T.

The President's Department of Protection from Extraordinary Supernatural Threats

To:

From:

TOP SECRET

Re: Operation Riding Hood

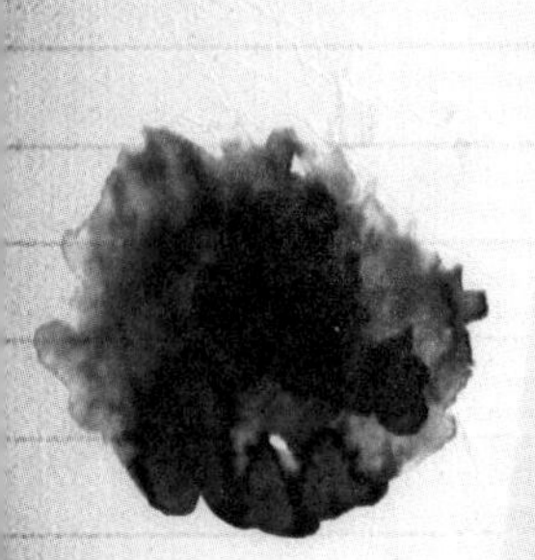

Dear Mr. President,

Please be notified that P.E.S.T. has identified and confirmed Threat A7GH Alpha. There is a dirty great werewolf on the loose in Washington, D.C.

Gulp.

The attached photograph was taken by Agent last night. Please note the White House with a full moon in the background, and, of course, the massive werewolf leaping towards the camera. P.E.S.T. will proceed with Operation Riding Hood. We are bringing in Van Helsing.

Yours,

PS: Agent 's funeral is next Wednesday.

MYTH 2:

Werewolves Only Change When There Is a Full Moon

WRONG. A werewolf can change at any time it chooses, though it has no choice about transforming when the **moon** is full. At this time of the month, a few decide to protect their secret by chaining themselves up in a strong cage. Most, however, simply prefer to gobble up anyone who sees them.

MYTH 3:

A Dead Werewolf Turns Back into a Human

WRONG. A werewolf that is slain in its wolf form stays in its wolf form, which is just as well - it could be tricky for the slayer to explain why they are standing over Auntie Pam's dead body with a crossbow in hand. Also, very few people want a hat made from Auntie-Pam skin.

MYTH 4:

Being Bitten by a Werewolf Will Turn You into One

WRONG. A werewolf never, ever stops at **ONE** bite. What's left of its victim couldn't turn into a were-hamster. In fact, werewolf blood runs in families, though it is never possible to tell who will be struck by the curse. The affliction may stay hidden for hundreds of years before a werewolf's great-great-great-great-granddaughter suddenly finds herself with a litter of very hairy babies.

How to Spot a Werewolf

The **true horror** of the werewolf is that to the untrained eye, it looks just like a normal person. Anyone might be a werewolf, as **Little Red Riding Hood**[4] found out. But although the werewolf may look like your **sweet**, rosy-cheeked grandmother who has false teeth and only ever seems to eat mashed potatoes and oatmeal, don't be fooled. Inside, it will *always* be thinking about chomping on its next victim. Most werewolves have learned to hide their secret well, but the mark of the beast cannot be hidden from the keen slayer.

There are many **signs** to look for.

[4] The story of Little Red Riding Hood was rewritten because the true tale was too scary. What actually happened was that the grandmother's teeth were all the better to eat her with. Little Red Riding Hood ended up as lunch, while granny burped happily and had a coffee.

Hair

Keep an eye out for people with **thick, glossy** manes and those who have a lot more body hair than usual. A full beard on a woman is normally a dead giveaway, though, for reasons not yet scientifically understood, female social studies teachers also tend to grow thick beards. In addition to hairiness, the slayer **MUST** collect extra evidence. Some perfectly normal people – as well as social studies teachers – are naturally quite hairy.

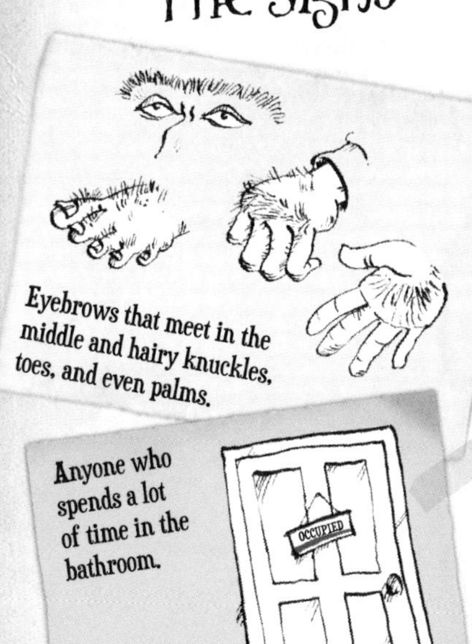

Eyebrows that meet in the middle and hairy knuckles, toes, and even palms.

Anyone who spends a lot of time in the bathroom.

People who own a lot of razors, shaving cream, aftershave, hair removal creams, tweezers, and – in extreme cases – garden shears.

Glove wearers.

VAN'S TIP: Do NOT slay someone just because they have shiny hair: they may have just stepped out of the hair salon.

Ears

The werewolf has extremely sharp hearing and even in human form can hear a **dog whistle** or a **pin drop.** Its ears are always a little more pointed than most humans' and may be hairy even if the rest of the body isn't. Always check closely, especially on cold days. Attacking people who are wearing fur earmuffs can lead to unpleasant misunderstandings.

VAN'S TIP: A dog whistle is the slayer's friend. The sound it makes is too high for humans to hear but not for a werewolf's ears. Blow one, and see if anyone turns around. Also, try saying "woof" very quietly and watching for a reaction.

Silver

Werewolves **HATE** silver. It is one of the few things that can kill them. Even the touch of it will make their **skin sizzle** like a frying pan full of bacon. No werewolf will have silver in the house.

Anyone who crosses the road to avoid a jewelry shop.

People who refuse to shake hands if you are wearing a silver ring.

Common excuses include a sudden need to go to the bathroom, remembering they left the oven on, and pretending they have an infectious skin disease and/or a fear of hands.

Food

Even in human form, werewolves find it difficult to resist raw flesh. However, most will have trained themselves to nibble the occasional carrot to disguise their ghastly appetites. Nevertheless, all werewolves would prefer meat for every meal, preferably so raw that it is still moving.

VAN'S TIP: Suspect someone is a werewolf but not certain? Serve them a raw steak for lunch, and see what happens. Look for growling and sudden hair growth. Be VERY careful – you may be next on the menu.

Breath

Unlike in the fairy tale, a **werewolf** cannot huff and puff and blow your house down, but its **breath** can stink up the place so badly that even pigs will be running for the exits. It is worse when it is in werewolf form, but the revolting stench never completely goes away.

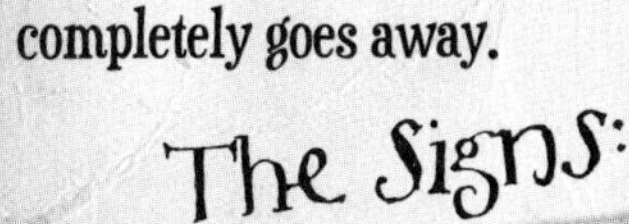

Those who talk with one hand covering their mouth.

Plants and flowers withering as someone walks past.

Mint suckers, mouthwash garglers, and frequent teeth brushers.

Howling

Few werewolves are **stupid** enough to be caught out this way, but all will have a strong urge to **howl** at the moon even if it is **not** full.

People who appear jumpy or nervous when the moon is visible. They may also say things like, "Good evening, how ar-oooooo?"

Anyone wearing dark glasses at night.

The Werewolf Transformation

The **metamorphosis** of a werewolf is a ghastly process that takes about **three minutes.** It involves a lot of grunting and snarling and some awful smells. It's best to hold your **nose**.

VAN'S TIP: Werewolves are helpless during the early stages of transformation and therefore easy to slay. Though you might be thought of as a bit of a wimp.

Stage 1

The first thing to change is the werewolf's breath. It is never minty fresh but now it will start to stink like a mixture of old dead things and dirty toilets, with a dash of sweaty feet.

Stage 2

Fingernails quickly grow into sharp claws. Thick, rough fur sprouts all over the body, including the face and hands.

Stage 3

An interesting stage. Halfway through the transformation, the semiwerewolf will drop to all fours, bones cracking as its body changes, and start sniffing its own rear end. This can be awkward at parties.

Stage 4

The werewolf will tear off its now too-tight clothes with its new claws. It will drool as its teeth lengthen into fangs. If you value your life, this is a very good time to run away screaming.

Stage 5

Known scientifically as the "Ugh, that's disgusting" stage, during the final part of the transformation, the nose stretches into a muzzle with a painful, wet grinding sound, while the ears prick up, already listening for prey.

Know Your Enemy: The Complete Werewolf

So what does the transformed werewolf really look like? All will now be revealed.

Muscles

The werewolf has greater strength than any man or wolf. It can run all night, leap over any wall, and tear a small building apart in under seven minutes. Imagine what it can do to its victims!

Claws

As sharp as razors and as strong as steel, these claws can rip through almost anything, including armor, doors, and – as I have found out – even the sturdiest pants.

Ears

Pointed, large, and able to hear an ant blowing its nose across a desolate moor.

Eyes

The werewolf can see in the dark, which is a tiny bit of a pain in the neck for anyone trying to hide.

Nose

This outstanding nose is supersensitive (which can be used to your advantage – see Chapter 4). The werewolf can track down a cocktail sausage from twenty miles away.

Face

In a word: ugly. This is NOT a face you want to see staring through your window in the middle of the night. Some victims die of fright as soon as they see a werewolf. They are the lucky ones.

Jaws and Teeth

Usually drooling and blood-stained, the werewolf's powerful jaws can bite through steel. It can gobble a large chicken with a single snap of its needle-sharp teeth.

Chapter 3

The Werewolf World

Unfortunately, **werewolves** can be found all over the world. They have spread like **Cousin Olga's** athlete's foot and come in many shapes and sizes – all of them more ghastly than a hat full of scorpions. The horrible creatures have adapted to live in most places and are found everywhere.

I have hunted great shaggy werewolves in the mountain villages of the **Himalayas** and have *been* hunted by sleek, deadly Nagual werewolves in the jungles of South America. What you need to remember is: the wise slayer knows everything about their prey. Knowing your **Mexican** Nagual from your melancholy **Swedish** werewolf might mean the difference between life and death.

Where Do Werewolves Come From?

How and when the first werewolf appeared is something of a mystery, even to me. Nevertheless, I have a theory: Long, long ago, when humans were more grunty, they decided the noble wolf would make a suitable pet.[5] This meant that over hundreds of years, wolves changed from intelligent, strong, **silent night hunters** into yappy little fluff-balls begging for scraps, chasing sticks, and wearing collars around their neck and ribbons in their hair.

The real wolves that remained saw their brothers and sisters begging from the table and licking faces, and became very angry. In **revenge**, they took small children (this is why there are so many old stories about children being raised by wolves) and began changing them. Humans had turned wolves into dogs, and now wolves created **wolf-humans**, keeping them in their wild world for so long that the children grew hairy and powerful and deadly. Then they sent them back to hunt. The werewolf had been **born!**

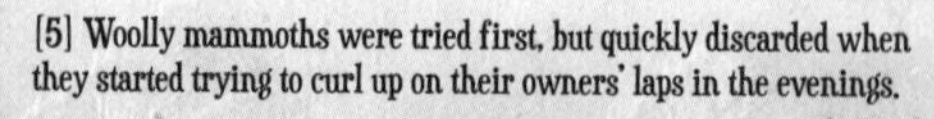
[5] Woolly mammoths were tried first, but quickly discarded when they started trying to curl up on their owners' laps in the evenings.

There are, of course, other theories about how **werewolves** first came into being. For many years, I have enjoyed collecting them as part of my library.

Take a look at this piece, for example:

I found this **Ancient Egyptian** papyrus while hunting down a werewolf in the **tombs** and pyramids of **Cairo.** It shows the wolf-headed god **Fi-Do** laying a curse on a man who had stolen the god's bone of power. The curse turned the thief into the first werewolf. It was later killed by a slayer whose name - if my translation of the ancient hieroglyphics is correct - was **Vanhelsis the Mighty.**

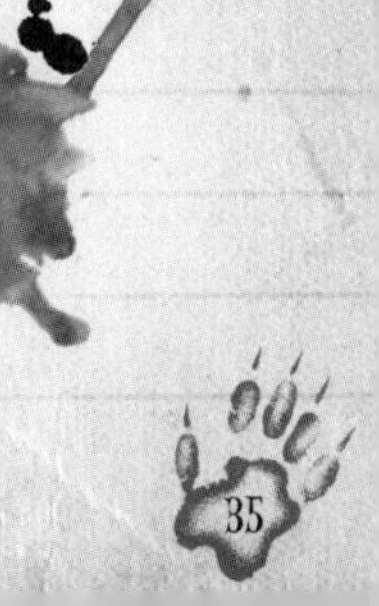

And there's this old parchment that I discovered in the library of the University of Dummköpf and forgot to take back.[6]

Hark ye to this warning and beware the beast that has killed. It hunts me. Through the night, every night, it hunts me.

My people made the mistake of making war upon a tribe called the Lunatix. We slayed them all, or thought we did, but our chief was killed in battle. His only son, Ethelred the Flower-Arranger, become our new chief. Instead of battle and glory, Ethelred preferred long walks in the countryside and baking cakes. We begged the gods to make him strong and fierce like his father. The gods answered – a druid came to our village. One stormy night, beneath a full moon, this mysterious spell-weaver sacrificed a wolf and performed a powerful ritual of dark magic.

Afterwards, Ethelred seemed no different, but the druid told us to wait.

At the next full moon, Ethelred the Flower-Arranger became Ethelred the Wolf. No longer did he want cake.

I and the druid escaped his terrifying

the druid had gone I found a note fr

[6] Please do not mention this to the university librarian, a
I would have to sell both kidneys, a lung, and my right arm to pay the fine

The story ends there but with it was another, shorter, parchment. . .

Ha ha ha HA HA.

How do you like Majiktrix

How do you like your Stupid chief now, eh?

Ha Ha Ha HA HA!

Majiktrix

Druid of the Lunatrix tribe

WEREWOLVES OF THE PAST

However the werewolf first came into existence, we know one thing for sure: throughout history, there have been many recorded outbreaks, and – I am proud to say – the **Van Helsing family** has always been on hand to help. You are in safe hands, dear reader, just look at the evidence...

A letter sent by my Great-Great-Great-Great-Aunt Grünhilde from Poligny in France.

My dearest darling Horst,

What a dreadful time it has been for a feeble and frail woman like your poor Grünhilde! I declare, traveling these terrible roads has left me as tired and weak as a kitten. And then, a werewolf attack. And I was wearing my new dress!

The horrible, horrible creature sprang at me with hunger in its glowing red eyes – just like old Johann Bömfur at the Winter Ball last year. Then it put one of its nasty, dirty paws on my dress. I'm afraid your sweet, timid little Grünhilde became quite angry. I punched the ghastly thing in the throat, then broke its knee with a tiny kicky-wicky.

As it lay there howling, I jumped up and down on its head. Not very ladylike, I know, but silk is soooo very difficult to get clean.

Your loving

Grünhilde

August 1521

VAN'S NOTE: I have seen portraits of Great-Aunt Grünhilde. She was the size of a small building and could carry a cow under each arm.

Then there was the infestation of werewolves in the German town of Griefswald in 1640.

This page comes from my great-**great**-**great**-**grandfather's** diary.

Journal of Munter Van Helsing

November 16th, 1640

Arrived in the town of Griefswald. Disgusting wolf vermin haunt every street and alleyway. No citizen is safe. Why, I had to slay three just getting from my carriage to the inn! Slayed two more of the pestilential beasts howling beneath my window. How is a man to sleep?

November 17th, 1640

Once again the immense Van Helsing brain has found a solution. I asked the people of Griefswald to bring me every scrap of silver within the town. Luckily, I brought Wolfshredding Wanda, my trusty gun. Today, we made bullets. Tonight I hunt. Received a letter from Agnes. Her ankles are playing up again.

November 18th, 1640

I have returned home. Griefswald is clean of wolves. (Note: the line "Well, that was another howling success," after I had killed the beasts caused many admiring laughs – use again.) What remained of the silver seems to have accidentally fallen into my luggage. Carriage jingles!

What's this? Oh, yes, a page from "Gibbering" Olaf Van Helsing's notebook.

London, May 5, 1725

Ah ha! They said I was mad, but I have discovered the werewolf's greatest weakness! It is cheese! It burns them. Oh, how it burns them. I have built a giant trap made entirely of cheese and made myself weapons of cheese. Now it comes.

It is here! It has entered the trap.

Oh.

We don't talk about **Uncle Olaf** much but family legends say he wasn't really a Van Helsing at all. The story goes that he was found as a baby in the smoking remains of a mad **scientist's** castle. The Van Helsings adopted him, but he never really got the hang of the family business.

THE WORLD OF WOLVES

Unfortunately, there are very few corners of the world that are free of the werewolf curse, and the slayer's work is never done. They're like washing the dishes - just when you think you've finished them, they start piling up again, and they only get worse the longer you leave them. Slay one in **Italy** and two will pop up in **Tasmania**. Clean up **London** and an infestation will break out in **New York**.

There are many different kinds of werewolf, and the slayer who wants to stay alive will be familiar with all of them. Here's what you need to know:

KITSUNE

(say: kit-soo-nay)

Found in Japan and China, Kitsune are more were-*foxes* – they are born foxes and turn into humans. They are more attractive than true werewolves (what isn't?), smaller, and can be vicious. Myths say they can grow up to nine tails, athough I have never met a Kitsune with more than one. This is a pity, as their tails make excellent dusters.

HOW TO SPOT A KITSUNE

• Like normal werewolves, Kitsune in human form are unusually hairy, though sleeker, and have white patches.

• Look for a fox-shaped shadow, or a foxy reflection in mirrors. Or a funny-looking lump in the back of their pants: Kitsune don't always lose their tails when they take human form.

• Kitsune hate dogs, so always carry a Chihuahua in your pocket.

SLAYING A KITSUNE

Kitsune like to play cruel tricks on their victims rather than just eating them right away. You can easily put a stop to this with a large axe.

LOBISÓN

(say: low-bee-son)

A particularly repulsive-looking creature with great hunched shoulders and, often, a large mustache, the Lobisón can be found across Argentina and Brazil. The Lobisón eats mostly dead things, giving it the worst breath of any werewolf. I have slayed only one and that was a difficult hunt, mainly because it is impossible to get within a hundred feet of the beast without fainting from its stench. I had to sneak up on it in a hot-air balloon.

HOW TO SPOT A LOBISÓN

- Most of the normal rules apply, but the Lobisón likes the taste of rotting meat in particular. Keep a sharp eye out for people lurking around trash cans behind restaurants.
- The Lobisón often hangs out in graveyards. Be careful how you slay: that group of people wearing black might just be there to bury granddad.

SLAYING A LOBISÓN

Keep upwind and use *very* long-range weapons, a rifle, or a guided missile if you have one handy.

LOUP GAROU

(say: loop gar-oooo)

Ooh la la! The Loup Garou is a French werewolf and similar to the classic werewolf, except for one or two small differences. In wolf form, the Loup Garou will eat as many as five or six people in one night, plus a fruit salad. After turning back into a human, it will be weak and faint for some time. It also burps frequently.

HOW TO SPOT A LOUP GAROU

- Loup Garous have bristles beneath their tongues. One way of checking is to kiss them, but this is NOT recommended: you may lose your lips. Disguise yourself as a dentist instead.
- Watch for anyone who looks as if they have eaten too much the night before and is grumpy in the morning, although, in France, this means almost everyone.

SLAYING A LOUP GAROU

If you know the name your werewolf uses when human, the Loup Garou can be cured by saying it three times to its wolf form, while striking it gently on the head with a knife. I have found that keeping quiet and striking it extremely hard on the head with a large axe works just as well.

NAGUAL

(say: na-wall)

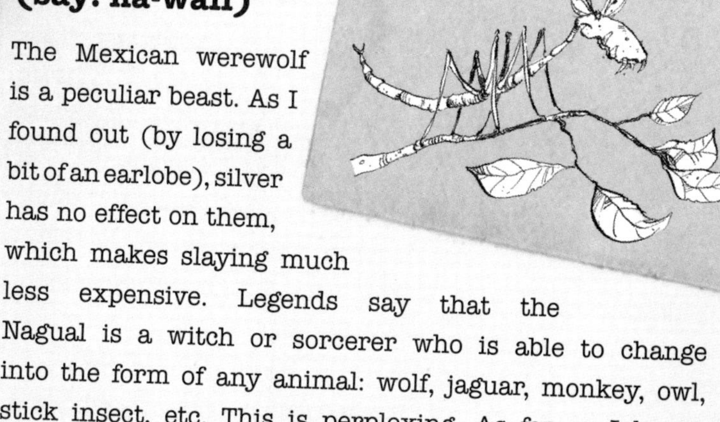

The Mexican werewolf is a peculiar beast. As I found out (by losing a bit of an earlobe), silver has no effect on them, which makes slaying much less expensive. Legends say that the Nagual is a witch or sorcerer who is able to change into the form of any animal: wolf, jaguar, monkey, owl, stick insect, etc. This is perplexing. As far as I know, no one has ever had their throat ripped out by a were-stick insect, but stranger things have happened.[7]

HOW TO SPOT A NAGUAL

- The Nagual witch or sorcerer transforms into a beast only during the night while sleeping. If you see anyone sleeping at night, add them to your list of highly suspicious characters.
- A few Naguals are proud of their ability and don't even *try* to keep their grisly secret. It's worth asking everyone you meet, "Hey, are you a disgusting fiend that stalks the night as a beast?"

SLAYING A NAGUAL

Any normal weapon will slay a Nagual, plus fire, holy water, and stones. If you meet a Nagual who has transformed into a snail, you can just step on it.

[7] I was once attacked by a possessed carpet.

SKIN WALKER

The North American Skin Walker terrorizes Native Americans and is a magical human who can change into any animal it likes, though the wolf form is a favorite. It is also able to transform into other people, which the Navajo Indians call "face stealing."

Unfortunately, it is also very good at arm stealing, leg stealing, and head stealing. These horrors like to cast evil spells, using tarantulas, rattlesnakes, and squirrels in their foul magics.

HOW TO SPOT A SKIN WALKER

• Skin Walkers have a yellow tinge to their skin, which, thankfully, makes them easy to spot. They will try to disguise this, and so be suspicious of anyone with a bag on their head.

• Keep an eye out for anyone carrying spiders, snakes, and squirrels in their handbag.

SLAYING A SKIN WALKER

Only a bullet covered in white ash will slay a Skin Walker, so keep a pocketful of ash handy.

EIGI EINHAMR

(say: eye-gee ein-hammer)

Meaning "not of one skin," the Eigi Einhamr can be found in Norway, Sweden, and Denmark and is said to transform into a werewolf when it wears the skin of a wolf. This is complete nonsense! I own several wolfskin hats and a wolfskin coat, as well as wolfskin pants, gloves, and underwear, and *I* have never turned into a wolf.

In fact, the Eigi Einhamrs are just common werewolves trying to be different and can be spotted and slain as normal. They are miserable creatures who like nothing better than a good moan. Typical. With werewolves it's all about me, me, me. Slaying them soon puts them out of everyone's misery.

Canadian werewolves are a peculiar mix of Loup Garou and the common European werewolf. Unusually friendly and polite, they make their victims feel comfortable and welcome before eating them.
Greenland
Canada
USA
Werewolves in Greenland are protected by their thick fur coats and don't mind the cold. They do get tired of eating polar bears all the time though.
South America is full of werewolves, and they have many different names. Some of them - like Tlahuelpuchi - are so difficult to pronounce that people have been known to choke to death while trying to scream, "Help, help, I'm being attacked by a Tlahuelpuchi."
Brazil
Argentina
There is evidence that werewolves originated in Africa, but the whole continent is mysteriously free of them now. Some people think this is due to some work of great magic by African slayers in the past. Others think it is because elephants sat on them all.

Russia
China
Werewolves avoid India as the victims available there are "too spicy" for their tastes.
Australia
There are very few Australian werewolves, mainly because any creature running around at night with no shoes on is almost certainly going to step on a poisonous snake or insect, or a crocodile.

Chapter 4

The Complete Slayer

Now it is time to learn how to fight your enemy! Soon, you, too, can be a world-saving hero like me: bold, dashing, and just a little bit fearsome. Of course, being a **slayer** is not just a job, it is also a *lifestyle*. You will be always on duty, ready to step in when peril threatens and danger rears its repulsive, drooling head.

You're sure you want to be a slayer? It is not yet too late. You can still put this book down and take up a job that is less **dangerous** - lion-taming or tiger-juggling, perhaps.

If you're sure, many changes await you. Look how I changed from a **pimply lad** in embarrassing leather shorts to a slaying **hero**. Those were the days: up at sunrise, running through the forests of Grüselighausen to improve my stamina, lifting weights to improve my strength, and hunting to improve my… err… hunting. Quickly, I grew fit. My muscles bulged. My teeth twinkled. The young women of Grüselighausen swooned when they saw me, and the men all wished to shake my hand.

I learned many valuable lessons in those days.

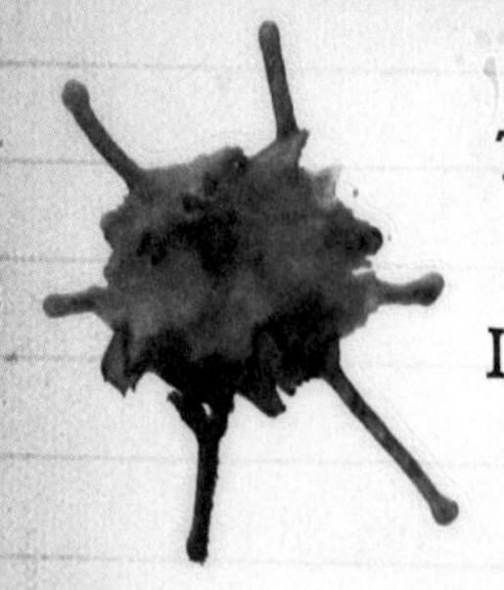

The first was the most important. The werewolf curse still hung heavy upon the town. Soon, I was ready to slay my second beast: **Herman Schnausermann**, the local bank manager. He was a small man with a bristly mustache, hairy legs, and a twitchy eye. I had long suspected him of being a werewolf. Several of the bank's customers had gone missing, and I had once seen him scratching his ear. "That's not unusual," you may say. "I scratch my ear all the time." **Yes, but do you do it with your toes?**

When the full moon arrived, I took an axe and waited outside the bank. Later, as I lay in bed with thirteen broken bones, a cracked skull, torn muscles, blood pouring from a dozen wounds, and a terrible case of fleas, I had plenty of time to think about that first valuable lesson. The lesson was this: jogging through the woods and doing a few push-ups does **NOT** make you a slayer. I had been lucky with Great-Aunt Hellga, but there was more work to do before I could slay Herman Schnausermann.[8]

[8] I learned my lesson well. The next time I saw him, it was through the cross-hairs of a very long-range crossbow.

What to Wear

Now we begin the most important part of your **transformation** into a slayer, starting with style...

"Huh?" you may say. "What does style matter to a slayer? Who cares what you wear as long as the job gets done?" This is foolish. As I found out on that long-ago day in Grüselighausen, the successful slayer cannot face their enemy wearing leather shorts that have grown far too small.

Neither can they say things like "Ummm... good evening, Mr. Schnausermann, sir. I've... errr... come to... ummm... slay you. If you don't mind. **Thankyousoverymuch.**" The werewolf simply chuckles under its breath while it watches its **claws** growing and glinting in the moonlight. And the slayer begins shaking and spluttering things like, "Or we could l-leave it u-until **t-t-tomorrow** if it's **i-inconvenient.** Should I make an appointment with your **s-s-secretary?"**

No, it is important that the werewolf is more terrified of you than you are of it. This means facing it with a certain style: dressed to impress, a twinkle in your eye, and a clever put-down on your lips. The werewolf is used to its victims **screaming**, **blubbering**, and tearing their own hair out with fear. An enemy who looks and acts as cool as a fridge full of **cucumbers** will confuse and frighten it.

The slayer will need to feel at home in many places - from stately homes and the offices of **world leaders** to misty, desolate moors. With a little thought, it is possible to be combat-ready while always looking confident and stylish. The look you are aiming for is **noble hero**.

VAN'S TIP: Pockets, pockets, pockets! Remember: weapons, maps, traps, and gizmos are all part of the slayer's inventory. You can never have too many pockets.

HAT: A knitted woollen hat might be nice and warm, but does it say "slayer"? No. Try something with a wide brim that can be pulled over the eyes. This can be a useful disguise and makes any slayer look dashingly mysterious.

VAN'S TIP: Black is good for camouflage and never goes out of fashion.

COAT: A long, black leather coat offers warmth and protection and can hide numerous useful pockets. Most importantly, it looks fabulous when you are standing in the moonlight, crossbow in hand, with the wind billowing it out behind you. A must-have for any serious slayer.

UNDERWEAR: For outdoor hunting, wear warm underwear. Also bear in mind that your clothes may be shredded by a werewolf's claws and teeth during that desperate fight to the death. It is difficult to look heroic when everyone can see you are wearing yesterday's underwear with little hearts all over them.

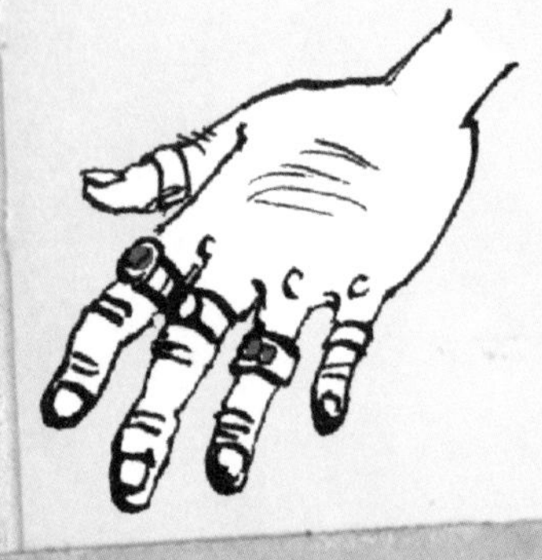

JEWELRY: Silver, obviously. I recommend that every slayer wears at least three or four rings. They're stylish and will cause any werewolf a massive amount of pain when you punch it in the face.

BOOTS: Some suppliers offer boots with hidden blades that spring out of the toecap. I have found these can go off by accident, tripping you up at awkward moments and – on one occasion – cutting off Lady Tuttlington's big toe during an energetic foxtrot at her Grand Summer Ball.

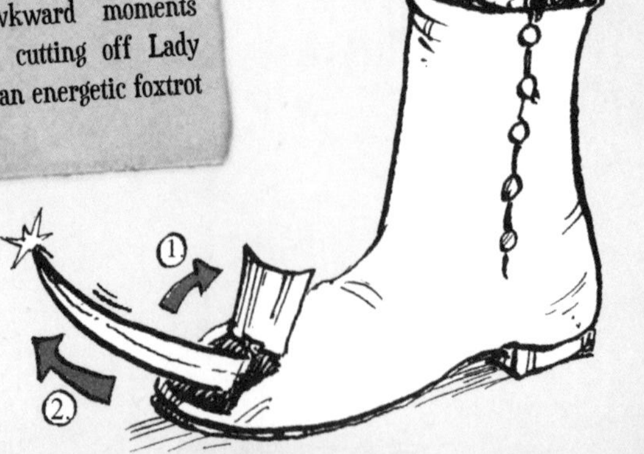

Talking to Your Prey

There is a saying among slayers: "Speak softly and carry a big axe, sword, crossbow, an assortment of guns, traps, explosives, and a **Hungarian gouging spoon.**" When facing your prey, you should always be ready with a few sharp, well-chosen words. This will show the werewolf that you are **unafraid.** Also, anyone watching will think you are the bee's knees.

Feel free to make up your own, but here are a few phrases I have used with great success.

"Down, boy!"
Works well just before slaying. Also, **"Bad boy! In your basket!"**

"Yes, I *get* it: growl drool snarl snarl howl snuffle howl. *Boring!*"
Roll your eyes and yawn while saying this. Then shoot.

"Fetch *this*."
As you fire a silver-tipped crossbow bolt.

"Looks like someone forgot to shave this morning. Let's see what we can do about that."
Say this as you draw your sword.

"My, what big teeth you have. Feel like picking them up off the floor?"
Follow this with a punch in the mouth.

VAN'S TIP: When talking to your prey, try to stand with the full moon or a burning building directly behind you. It won't make any difference to the werewolf's sharp eyes, but you will look devilishly dashing.

Equipment and Weapons

The best way to slay a werewolf is from a very, *very* long way away: sitting in a tree with a thermos of cocoa and a muffin, if you can. That isn't always possible, though, and the slayer should be expert with every kind of weapon. As you advance, you will discover which weapons, traps, and gizmos suit you best, but the basic slayer inventory should include the following:

Compass and Map

Always have these with you and learn how to use them! A slayer who wanders around lost on the desolate moor while the werewolf terrorizes a village ten miles away is a slayer who will be laughed out of town.

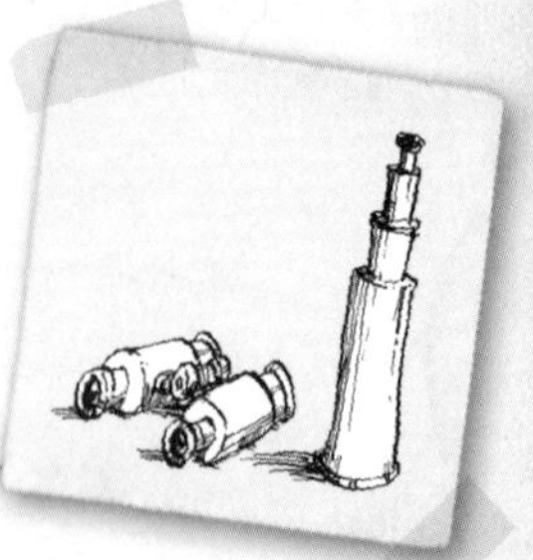

Telescope/Binoculars

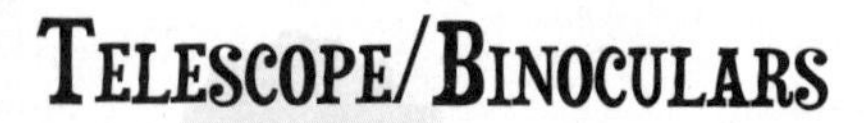

Werewolves have incredible eyesight; *you* have gadgets. Use them.

Sword

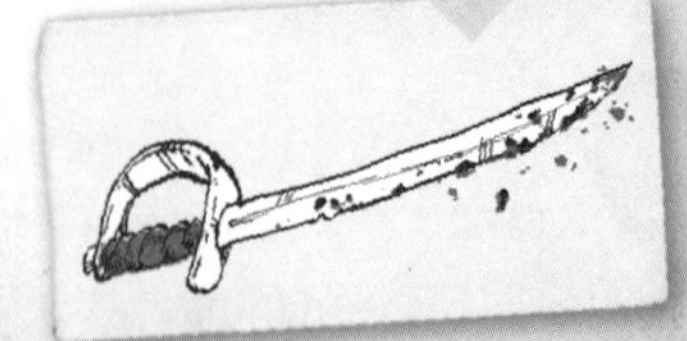

Werewolves may be difficult to harm with standard weapons and may heal amazingly fast, but even with its supernatural powers, any werewolf will find the loss of its head a major inconvenience.

Axe

The traditional tool for killing wolves, as approved by lumberjacks everywhere. All werewolves know this and will be terrified by the sight of a swinging axe. Plus, you can chop wood with it – very handy.

Silver Bullets

Guns are effective weapons, but silver bullets aren't cheap, so keep cost at the front of your mind as that huge, screaming fiend leaps at you from the darkness.

Crossbow

There are many different kinds of crossbows. Find one that is easy to carry, accurate, and powerful. Pay attention to styling: a good crossbow should be both a deadly weapon and a nifty accessory. Anyone watching should be left gasping in awe as you expertly drop a werewolf with a cool flick of the trigger.

Crossbow bolts should be tipped with silver and, again, this can get expensive. However, they can be easily found after you have slain your prey and reused: doing this with bullets can be messy.

Flaming Torch

As waved by many an angry villager, a flaming torch is a useful weapon. Werewolves don't particularly like fire, and for one good reason: their fur is very greasy. Touch a werewolf with a flaming torch and it will go up like a witch on a bonfire.

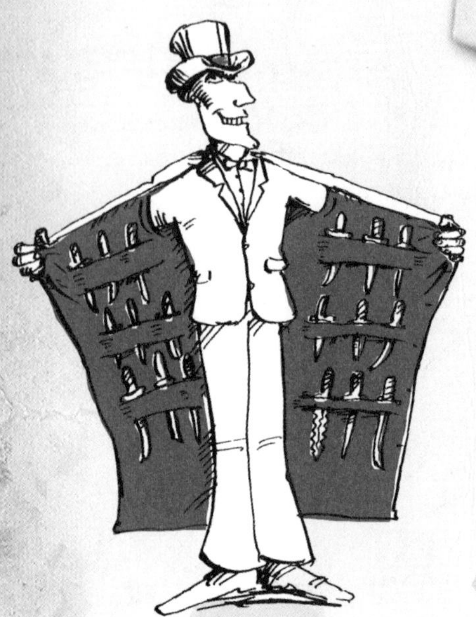

Silver-plated Pocket/Boot/ Sleeve Daggers

Keep a selection of secret daggers on you for hand-to-claw fighting and throwing. They are very handy for those "Ooops. I've dropped my weapon" moments.

Explosives

No slayer should venture out without Van Helsing's "Chewy Surprise" doggie treats and a stick of dynamite. Remember to bring matches, too: trying to light a fuse by rubbing two twigs together while a werewolf is charging at you can be annoying.

Traps and Gizmos

Always have a few surprises up your sleeve. There are many **gizmos** available, including superpowered sirens that will burst any werewolf's sensitive eardrums and wolf-hypnotizing sausages. Traps can range from pocket-sized gadgets to **enormous contraptions**. Each has its place in the slayer's equipment. Setting up an elaborate trap with tripwires, explosives, and sharpened stakes can take time, but the end result will be worth it, and watching the werewolf walk into it will make a jolly night out for local children. Simple traps that should be carried at all times include...

Caltrops

These handy little gizmos are made of four sharp silver spikes. However you throw them, one spike will always land pointing upwards, just waiting for a werewolf to step on it. You'll hear it screaming from the other side of the desolate moor!

The Boulder

Find a heavy boulder and balance it on the edge of a cliff or steep hill, with just a small wedge keeping it in place. (Note: You may need to pay someone to help with this - make sure you add the expense to your bill.)

Attach a long piece of string to the wedge. Mark the spot where the boulder will fall, then leap around yelling, "Helloooo, tasty flesh right here. Come and get your tasty flesh, Mr. Hairy." When the werewolf reaches the spot you have marked, pull the string. You should now have an extremely flat werewolf. Job done.

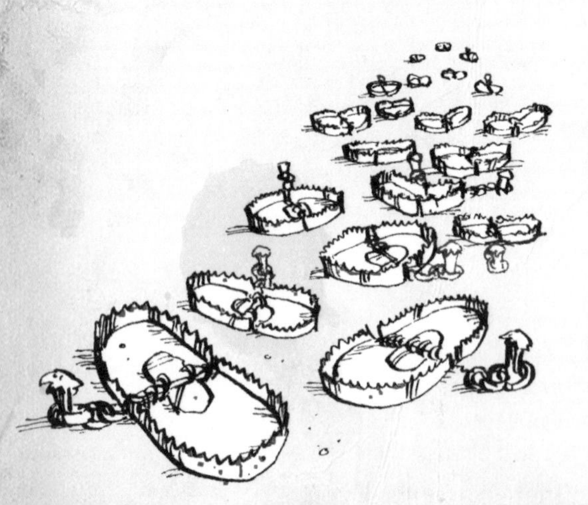

Bear Traps

A single bear trap won't slow a werewolf down for long, but I have had good results using twenty at a time.

The Exploding Chicken

Werewolves can't resist a plump, tasty hen, so why not serve one with extra-spicy stuffing? A high-quality exploding chicken (such as those sold by the Van Helsing Slayer Supplies and Equipment Company) will look and smell just like the real thing and will definitely leave a nasty taste in the mouth. They'll be scraping werewolf off the walls five miles away!

The Wolf Mangler

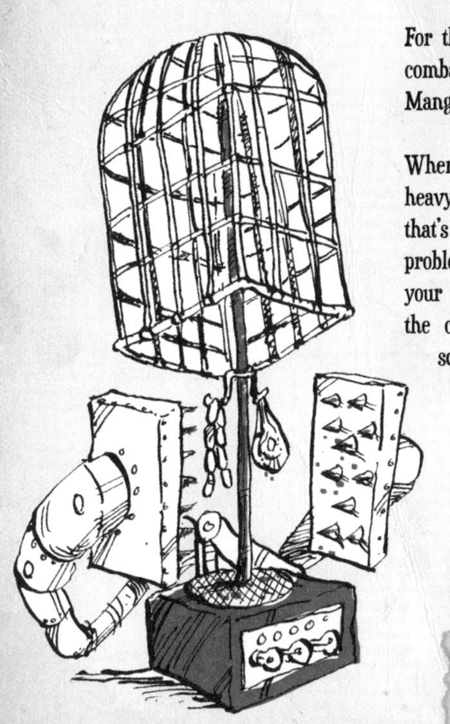

For the slayer who likes to avoid close combat, try the Van Helsing Wolf Mangler featuring FootPad technology.

When the werewolf steps on it, a heavy cage drops from above, but that's just the start of the werewolf's problems: the cage is electrified. As your werewolf yelps and crackles, the crushing mechanism is triggered, squashing your werewolf into a small cube. Finally, a small drawer pops out, presenting its remains in a stylish and eye-catching cup, ready for your trophy room or mantel.

VAN'S TIP: Do NOT use the Wolf Mangler in built-up areas.

Check the **Van Helsing Slayer Supplies and Equipment Company** catalog for all the latest in fun and exciting gadgets at low, low prices - you'll wonder how we do it!

Training

No matter how brave you are and how hip you look, a flabby, out-of-shape slayer is just a werewolf snack on two legs. However, training to slay these beasts can be tricky. Unless you are lucky enough to have a werewolf **trapped** in the basement, you can't practice fighting, and there is no way to prepare for that moment when you first come **face to hideous face** with one. Even so, your life will depend on your slayer skills and you should take every opportunity to keep them sharp. For instance, during breakfast, I stick a picture of a werewolf on the wall and throw butter at it. I also like to lurk by the front door armed with just a slice of toast to bring the mailman down.

Here's a sample training program, taken straight from my own journal:

4:30 a.m. - 6:00 a.m.: Healthy breakfast, shower, hairstyling, and dressing.

6:00 a.m. - 7:00 a.m.: Run, then hiding practice, followed by running and hiding practice.

7:00 a.m. - 9:00 a.m.: Stealth, camouflage, and hunting - sneaking, tracking, ducking behind things, general snooping around.

9:00 a.m. - 11:00 a.m.: Target practice - throwing daggers, throwing axes, bow, crossbow, bombs, and small cannons.

11:00 a.m. - 12:00 noon: Dealing with complaining neighbors, rebuilding the shed.

12:00 noon - 1:00 p.m.: Light lunch, hairstyling, and wardrobe maintenance.

1:00 p.m. - 3:00 p.m.: Strength training - weightlifting, wagon pulling, pig tossing.

3:00 p.m. - 5:00 p.m.: Weapons practice - with sword, dagger, spear, etc.

5:00 p.m. - 6:00 p.m.: Bandaging.

6:00 p.m. - 8:00 p.m.: Bear hunting followed by hand-to-hand combat training, with bears.

8:00 p.m. - 9:00 p.m.: A good dinner of bear stew.

9:00 p.m. - 12:00 midnight: Night stalking, navigating by the moon training, looking great by moonlight practice.

12:00 midnight: Hairstyling and bed.

Unarmed Combat

My advice about fighting with a werewolf without weapons is simple: **NEVER** fight with a werewolf without weapons. Nevertheless, there will be times when even the best prepared slayer will be forced to battle hand to claw. For these times, I have developed a fighting technique I call Van-jit-su. Practice daily, asking friends and family to be your opponent, or simply poke a gorilla with a stick until it attacks you. A complete course can be found in my excellent book, ***Van-jit-su Made Easy,*** available from the Van Helsing Slayer Supplies and Equipment Company.

The Origami Werewolf

This move is **simple** but **effective** and will leave the **werewolf** completely knotted.

1 As the werewolf leaps at you, grab it by its ears (remember to wash your hands later).

2 Pull down sharply so that its head is between its legs.

3 Reach down with one hand and pull its rear right paw up behind its neck (be careful of those claws!). Repeat with rear left paw.

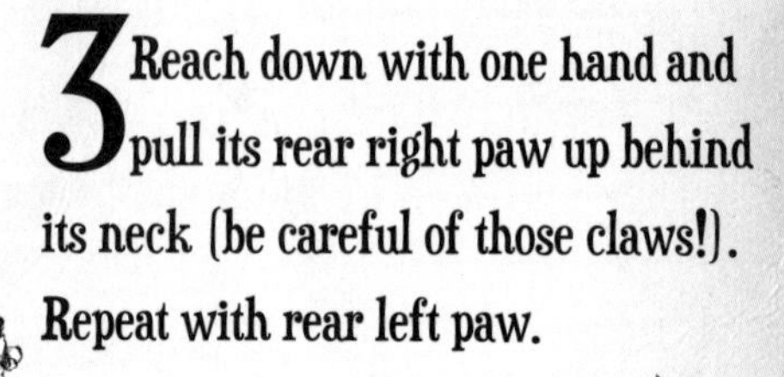

4 Taking its front right paw, insert into slot **A** (see diagram). Insert front left paw into slot **B**.

5 Your werewolf should now be in an "oven-ready chicken" position – unable to move and easy to slay.

The Striking Cobra

So, the **werewolf** has you pinned to the ground. **Drool** is **dripping** onto your face and it is just about to sink its **fangs** into your **throat**. Things don't look good but, in fact, you now have the **creature** at your **mercy**.

1 As the werewolf lowers its head to bite you, howling in triumph, bite its nose as hard as you can.

2 The werewolf's howl of triumph will quickly turn into a yelp of pain. Good. Do not let go. This is a great time to use one of those witty slayer phrases. I suggest, "Oo din see at oming, id oo?"

3 As the werewolf rears back, it will leave its nose between your teeth, and hop about in pain. You can now slay at your leisure. Remember to use lots of mouthwash later!

The Tail Spin

No animal likes having its tail pulled, and werewolves are no different. You will need strength and nerves of steel for this move but it's a doozy. The werewolf will be dazed, hurt, and left feeling a bit silly.

1 When the werewolf makes a lunge at you, dive between its legs, roll, and come to your feet behind it.

2 Quickly, grab it by the tail. (Note: If you are practicing with a friend or family member, ask them to tie a length of rope to their belt. **Do NOT** practice this move with the elderly or pets - slayers don't swing old people and kitties around, no matter how grumpy or annoying they might be.)

3 Keeping a tight grip and using all your strength, begin swinging the werewolf around in circles. At this point, it will be helpless, wondering if attacking a slayer was a very good idea and hoping that none of the other werewolves find out.

4 When the werewolf is spinning at a good speed, let go, preferably close to a wall or a large tree.

5 The beast will smash into the wall/tree headfirst. It will be stunned, allowing you to slay as and when you feel like it.

The Screaming "Van" Dash

This is one of my **favorite moves** and should be practiced every day. It has saved my life more times than I can count.

1 Point yourself in a direction away from the werewolf.

2 Move your legs in a pistoning motion as fast as you possibly can. Move **forward,** avoiding objects in your path. Try to imagine what will happen if the werewolf catches up with you – this will help you go faster.

3 Flap your hands above your head while screaming, **"WAAAAAAAAHHH!"**

4 Continue until you are far, far away from the werewolf.

Dos and Don'ts for the New Slayer

Here's a handy checklist that you can cut out and keep with you at all times...

DO

- Remember: training, training, training!
- Make sure your hair is looking good and your boots are polished. There's no excuse for sloppiness.
- Change your underwear frequently. You never know!
- Use plenty of deodorant. A werewolf can smell fear.
- Learn how to raise one eyebrow at times of great danger: it looks great.
- Be careful. No matter how confident you are, the werewolf is *always* a dangerous foe.
- Keep in mind that the werewolf is also hunting *you*. Keep one or two hidden weapons on you at all times, even in the bath.
- Be creative: everyday household items can be deadly in the right hands. I once slayed a werewolf with a stapler and a sponge.
- Spend some time each day thinking up witty remarks.
- Enjoy yourself. Just because you are the only thing that stands between humanity and these terrifying creatures doesn't mean you can't smile.

DON'T

- Get too clever. Why make a complicated plan involving kegs of gunpowder, candlelight, a hunchbacked assistant called Igor, and a small goat if a simple crossbow bolt will do?

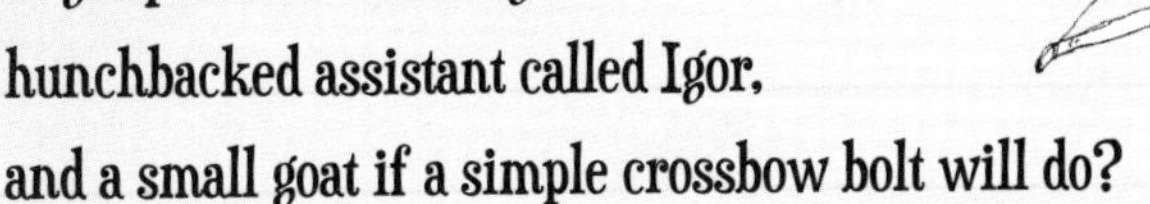

- Wear leather shorts. *Ever.*

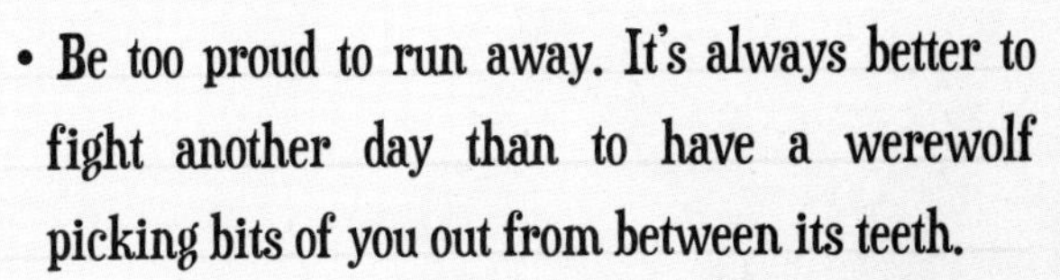

- Be too proud to run away. It's always better to fight another day than to have a werewolf picking bits of you out from between its teeth.
- Slay before you're absolutely sure your prey is a werewolf: it often leads to embarrassment.
- Talk too much. One witty remark is worth more than any amount of nervous blabbering.
- Use weapons you haven't practiced with. At best you'll just look silly, at worst you'll cut your own elbows off.

- Give up: the slayer *always* gets their prey.
- Forget to collect your reward.

Chapter 5

The Strategy of Slaying

Slaying can be a tricky business, and the slayer who doesn't use their brain is a slayer who will be wiped off the walls with a damp sponge.

However much you might want to, you cannot just walk up to someone and shoot him or her between the eyes with a **silver bullet**, no matter how large his or her mustache is.

As discussed earlier – and this is important – they might **NOT** be a werewolf, and people can be funny about that sort of thing. Secondly, if they are a werewolf, they will probably tear your arm off before you can pull the trigger. No, the slayer must always remember the two Ps: proof and planning. It may seem like a lot of unnecessary fuss and bother, but you must prove a werewolf is a werewolf and form a plan to deal with it quickly and professionally. Then you can move on to the one **D: death** – preferably the werewolf's.

VAN'S TIP: Try to avoid dying (unless it is part of a fiendishly clever plan). Death can slow even the best slayer down, and I should know – I have been pronounced dead three times. It stings a bit.

Finding a Werewolf

Werewolves are very good at staying hidden and making sure that no one who sees them lives to tell the tale. Finding one of these foul beasts can be like finding a burp in a hurricane. Once you have become a celebrity slayer like me, people will go down on their knees begging for your services. Until then, you'll have to go and find your own werewolves. There are two ways to do this.

Newspapers

Newspapers are the slayer's friend. Circle the dates of the full moon on your calendar and be on the lookout for stories of people disappearing or being horribly murdered immediately after those dates. The alert slayer may find other clues in the story, too. Look at this example...

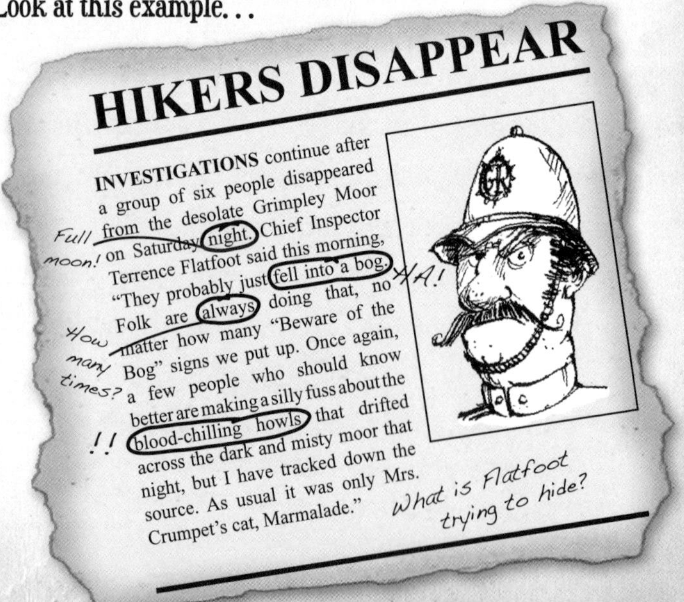

HIKERS DISAPPEAR

INVESTIGATIONS continue after a group of six people disappeared from the desolate Grimpley Moor on Saturday night. Chief Inspector Terrence Flatfoot said this morning, "They probably just fell into a bog. Folk are always doing that, no matter how many "Beware of the Bog" signs we put up. Once again, a few people who should know better are making a silly fuss about the blood-chilling howls that drifted across the dark and misty moor that night, but I have tracked down the source. As usual it was only Mrs. Crumpet's cat, Marmalade."

I did some quick research and found that over the past **10** years, more than **600** people had "fallen into a bog" on Grimpley Moor, including everyone who complained about howling. Mrs. Crumpet's cat, Marmalade, had died three years before. The culprit was, of course, a werewolf - none other than **Chief Inspector Terrence Flatfoot.**

ADVERTISING

As we have seen, few people believe that werewolves exist. Luckily for the slayer, however, they quickly start believing when one is snuffling at their front door. Anyone who has woken up to the sound of a spine-tingling howl or heard the blood-chilling screams of a werewolf's victims will quickly change their mind about werewolves being imaginary beasts and be desperate to find a slayer. You can make it easier for them to find you by placing advertisements in shop windows, newspapers, etc.

Paws in the Dirt

So, you've spotted signs of a werewolf infestation in the newspaper, or some terrified citizen has begged for your help, but how do you track your prey down? For such a large and smelly beast, the werewolf can be difficult to locate. It moves through the night as quickly and silently as a well-oiled weasel and its **supernatural senses** of smell and sight means it can easily detect when it is being followed. Once that happens, you might as well smear yourself with ketchup. However, hunting is an unavoidable part of the slayer's job.

Camouflage: By wearing black, the slayer should already be well camouflaged during nighttime missions. However, this will not stop the werewolf from smelling you. To disguise your scent, roll around in muck and leaves until you smell like the countryside. (If you are in the city, roll around in the gutter.) Horrible things will stick to your clothes. Your hairstyle will suffer. You will find things crawling out of your ears for days afterwards. Sometimes being a slayer comes at a terrible price.

SPEED AND STEALTH: Moving quickly and silently should be part of every slayer's daily training. You are aiming to be as silent as a ghost.[9] Avoid twigs snapping beneath your feet, and pay attention to your breathing – the werewolf will hear you if you start panting like a vampire in a garlic factory. Do NOT swear loudly when you fall into a stream.

PRINTS: Werewolves may slip through the night with cunning stealth but they are large, heavy beasts and will leave a trail of paw prints (and drool and blood) that can be followed by the sharp-eyed slayer.

[9] Not the kind of ghost that throws things around and screams "GETT OOOOOOUUUT" in people's faces when they move into a new house but the kind of ghost that glides silently through walls and wafts up to unsuspecting slayers while they are having a cup of chamomile tea before bedtime, making them spill it all down their pajamas.

HIDING (IN THE COUNTRYSIDE): Chasing a werewolf through the countryside can very quickly become being chased by a werewolf through the countryside. If that happens, hide. I've lost count of the times I have sat at the bottom of a slimy pond breathing through a reed. I can also recommend climbing a tree and wriggling down a rabbit hole. If you are lucky, you might later be able to leap out at the surprised werewolf shouting, "Coming, ready or not," as you take aim.

In the City

Like most other supernatural creatures, werewolves have adapted to living in the city. This presents the slayer with problems. Firstly, the slayer will not be able to follow paw prints over streets and sidewalks. Secondly, the werewolf will avoid crowds and travel through sewers, often making its secret lair in some stinking and forgotten underground hole. Some slayers may wish to follow their prey down a pipe filled with disgusting ooze, but they are on their own. My advice is to throw a couple of smoke bombs in the hole and wait until the werewolf surfaces.

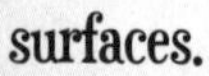

Planning and Tactics

Once you have found your werewolf, simply running at it swinging a huge axe and screaming **"AAAAAARGGHHH!"** is a certain way to end up in bite-sized chunks (it also looks silly). The successful slayer outsmarts the cunning werewolf. This means using your brain as well as your axe. Form your plan carefully, **paying attention** to every detail, and the battle is half won before it begins.

Secrecy

It is important to operate in complete secrecy. If the werewolf knows that it's being trailed by a slayer, it will be on its guard. Always have a variety of false noses and false identities on hand. The werewolf will take a keen interest in strangers, especially if they look threatening and/or tasty, so try to appear harmless as well as unappetizing. I often arrive in a werewolf-infested village dressed as a one-legged hobo (fewer legs for the werewolf to eat) or a big-nosed traveling washerwoman called Madame Winkleblötter, who looks so old and smelly that a werewolf would rather eat its own head than hers.

Maps and Charts

Whether it is a ruined castle, swamp, or stately home, always draw plans of your **battleground**. Pay special attention to places where you might wish to ambush the werewolf, marking any traps you set. Make sure that you show these to any confirmed nonwerewolf who may be wandering around. **Secrecy** is all very well, but I once had to scrape up the Count of Bavaria after he accidentally stepped in one of my **traps**. Annoyingly, this gave the werewolf time to **escape**.

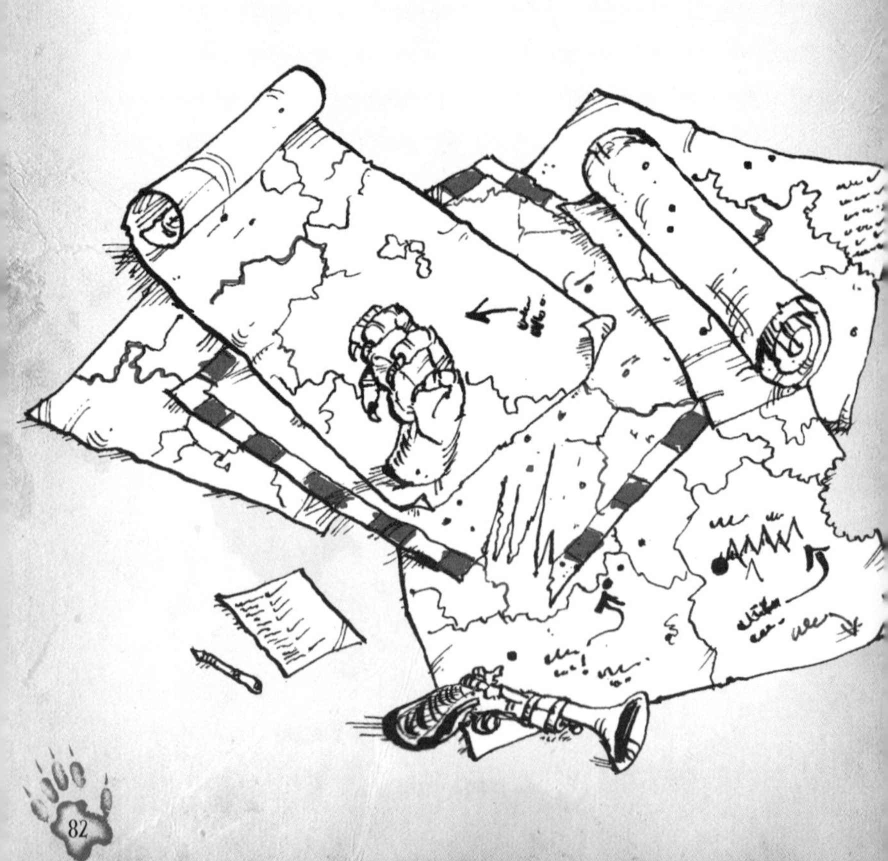

Choosing a Battleground

The time has come to face the beast, and it is important that you choose your position well. Here are a few things to consider.

1. *Can I block the entrance and booby-trap any of the werewolf's escape routes?* There's no point in luring a werewolf if it can just wander off whenever it feels like it.

2. *Do I have at least two escape routes?* You can soon be a long way away with a nice cup of tea and a piece of pie.

3. *Am I out of reach of the werewolf's claws/fangs?*[10] Remember: Going hand to claw with a werewolf = bad; shooting at it from a safe distance = good.

4. *How many traps can I lay between myself and the werewolf?* The more the better. By the time it reaches you, the werewolf should be in small, manageable chunks.

5. *Do I have a clear shot at it with my crossbow and silver bullets?* Hiding in the bathroom is not a good idea. Try to find a place where you can fire a few shots without putting yourself in any real danger.

6. *If I am using a screaming young person as bait, will he/she be safe?*[11]

[10] If battling in a large stately home, sitting in a chandelier high above the werewolf is ideal.
[11] Don't worry about this too much. Sometimes sacrifices must be made.

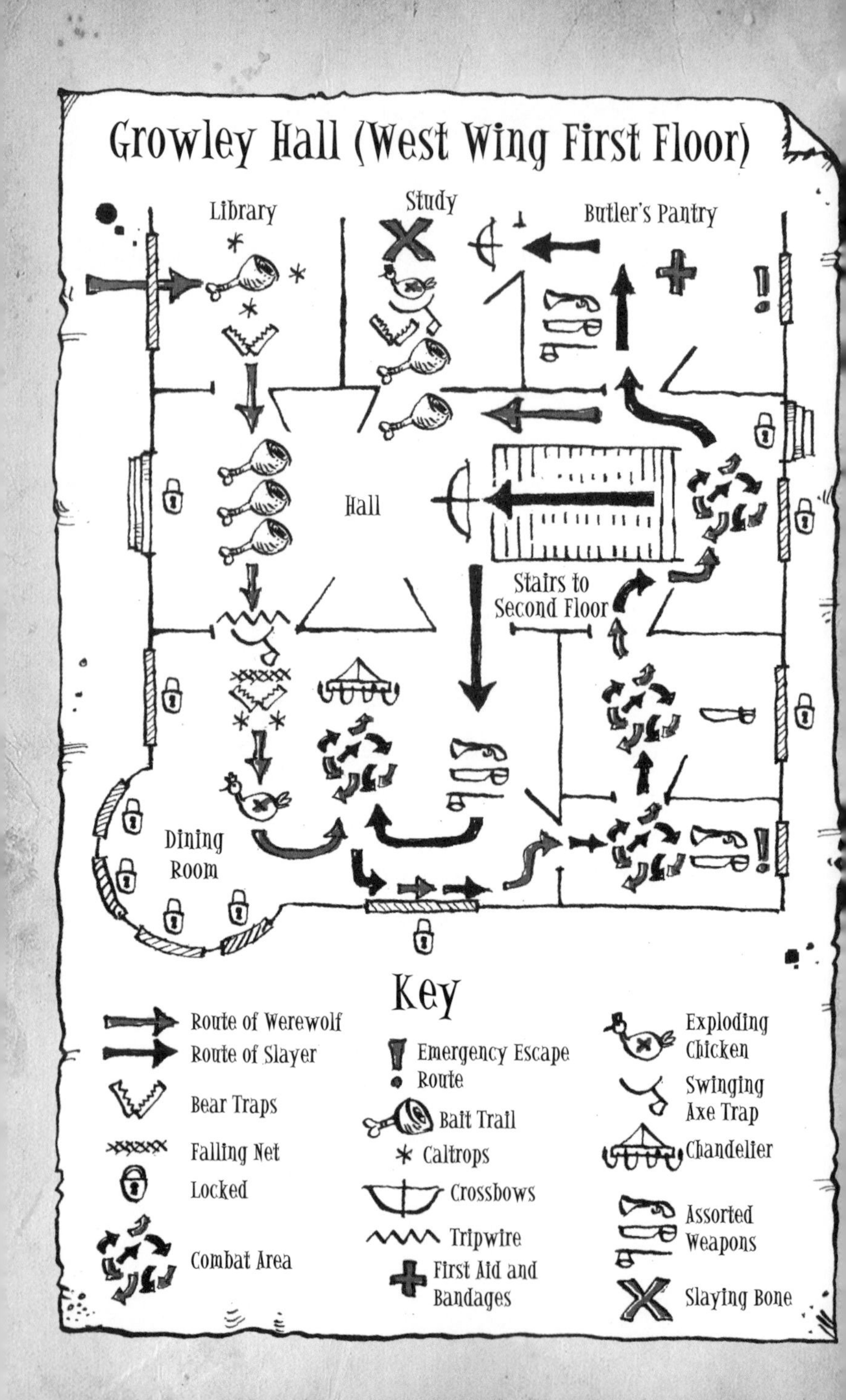
Growley Hall (West Wing First Floor)
Library
Study
Butler's Pantry
Hall
Stairs to Second Floor
Dining Room
Key
Route of Werewolf
Route of Slayer
Bear Traps
Falling Net
Locked
Combat Area
Emergency Escape Route
Bait Trail
Caltrops
Crossbows
Tripwire
First Aid and Bandages
Exploding Chicken
Swinging Axe Trap
Chandelier
Assorted Weapons
Slaying Bone

Lures and Bait

It is far, far better to bring the werewolf to you than to chase it across city and countryside (which is **tiring**, chilly, **mucky**, and time-consuming). Leave a trail of meat that leads to your clever trap *(tip: don't use live chickens - werewolves love them, but the chickens tend to wander off)* or - for even better results - use a **terrified** young lady wearing only her nightgown.[12] This is both traditional and effective. Try to choose someone who looks tender and juicy, and who screams well. Werewolves love a screaming victim.

If you cannot find a butcher shop or anyone idiotic enough to act as werewolf bait, try howling like a werewolf instead. Werewolves **protect** their territory fiercely and will **kill** any other werewolf muscling in. A good howl will have them bounding straight into your trap.

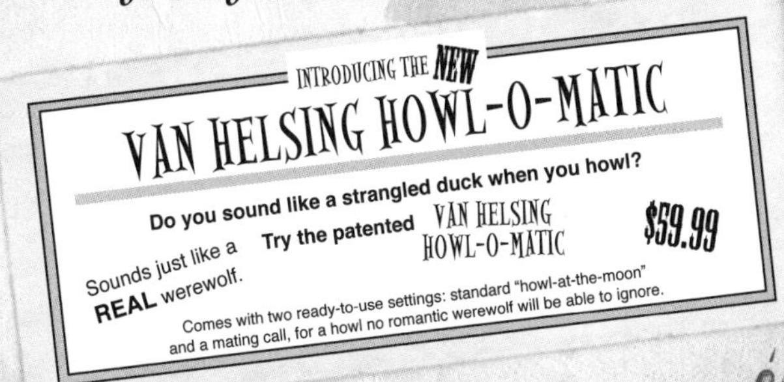

[12] A handsome young man wearing a T-shirt can be substituted if you are dealing with a *female* werewolf, as long as he is screaming.

Up Close and Personal

If you have planned well, you should not need to fight the werewolf hand to claw. Nevertheless, if you have an audience, they will expect a little close **combat**. Try to put on a show - leaping on tables and swinging from chandeliers always gets a few "**oohs**" and "**aaahs.**" For a successful slay, remember the following. . .

Keep your weapons in good working order. If your sword won't cut through butter, the chances are it won't cut through a werewolf either.

Don't be afraid to use any items that happen to be lying around: chairs, tables, and **priceless** antique vases; blazing logs from the fire; ornamental china kittens - most things can be used as a **weapon**. Try to use heavy/hard items - beating a werewolf to death with a pillow can be time-consuming.

A Trick Up Your Sleeve

Even the best plans sometimes go wrong, so never, never, never battle a werewolf without having a retreat option. For example, a few years ago I was fighting a particularly large and fearsome beast. One by one it survived all my traps. It had a dozen crossbow bolts sticking out of it and **bled** from a hundred wounds. Still the beast attacked, roaring in triumph as it fell on me, its teeth **gnashing** and its claws ripping at my pants.

Things did not look good.

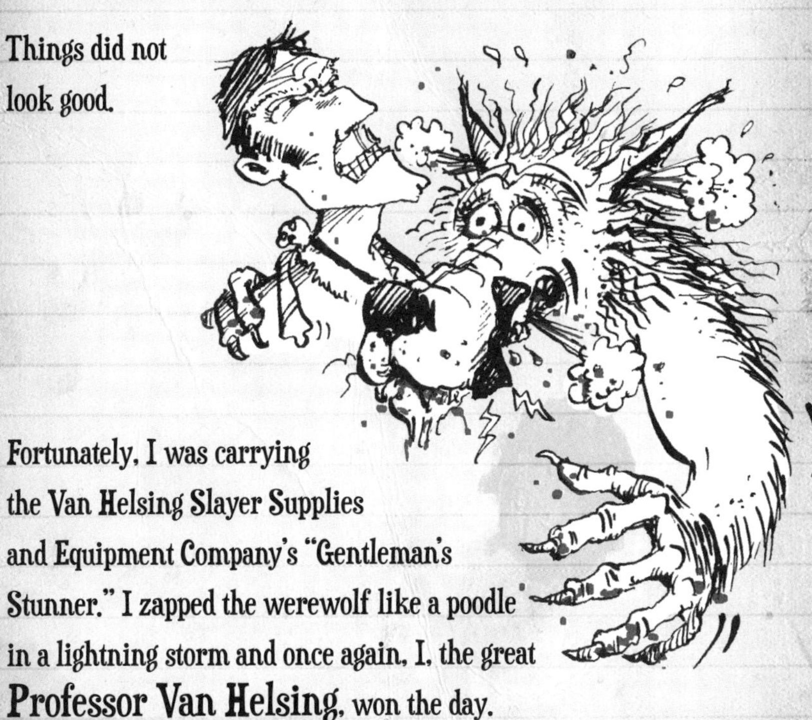

Fortunately, I was carrying the Van Helsing Slayer Supplies and Equipment Company's "Gentleman's Stunner." I zapped the werewolf like a poodle in a lightning storm and once again, I, the great **Professor Van Helsing**, won the day.

Strengths and Weaknesses

Yes, the werewolf is big and bad enough to make even the bravest person go running to mommy. But, however strong the werewolf might be, it will have weaknesses, too. The intelligent slayer aims to overcome the beast's strengths while taking full advantage of the chinks in its armor. (Note: Not actual armor. If you see a werewolf wearing armor – run!)

Strengths

Teeth

In a word: nasty. Keep clear of these or - even better - get rid of them. With the Van Helsing Slayer Supplies and Equipment Company's "Silver Jaw Breaker" boxing glove (or even just a large hammer), the slayer can make sure the werewolf will be eating its next meal through a straw.

Claws

It is difficult to declaw a werewolf during a fight, and you would probably ruin your nail clippers. Don't even try. Instead, simply chop the beast's paw off with a sharp sword or axe. You'll no longer have to worry about claws, and the werewolf will be seriously annoyed.[13]

Ears

Extremely sensitive. This can be turned to your advantage, however. Set off a loud siren,[14] and watch your deafened werewolf squeal.

Eyes

The werewolf has extremely good eyesight, so a poke in the eye should be one of the slayer's favorite tricks. The effects are immediate and spectacular. A blind werewolf is an easy-to-slay werewolf. Don't forget to swirl your finger around a bit!

Weaknesses

Heart

It's the bull's-eye of werewolf slaying. No living creature can shrug off a crossbow bolt to the heart.

Brain

The werewolf is a fiercely intelligent beast but will be unable to think clearly with a silver bullet rattling around inside its head.

Wolfsbane

Werewolves are immune to most poisons, except wolfsbane, which will melt them from the inside out until all that is left is a stinking pool of bubbling green goo. Very entertaining. The attractive plant with its dazzling blue flowers is easy to grow. Boil up a few and use it on the tips of arrows and crossbow bolts, or fry a steak in it and leave it out for your werewolf to discover.[15]

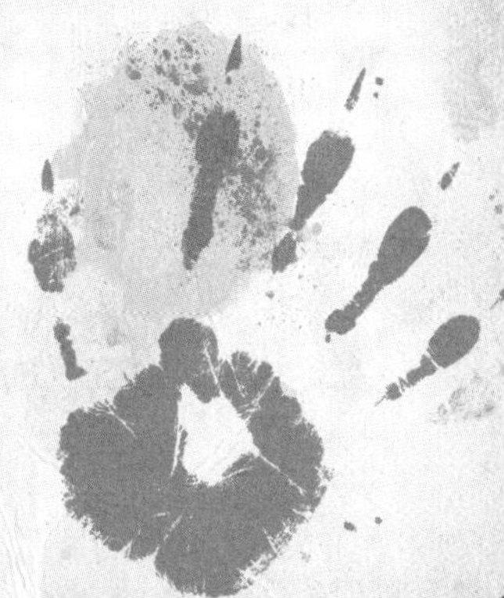

[13] With no paws, the werewolf will be sliding around like a camel on an ice rink and much less likely to escape.

[14] Such as the Van Helsing Ear Splitter (only $24.99 - a bargain).

[15] Wolfsbane also looks lovely in any flower arrangement, and just the scent will keep werewolves away.

The Pack

The last words of my dear old Great-Grandfather, Leopold Van Helsing, were, "Oh dear, I didn't know they came in packs, aaaargghhhh. . . !" Werewolves usually hunt alone but not always. There are few things as scary as a whole pack of werewolves bounding towards you, their great jaws hanging open and hunger burning in their eyes. At times like these, you'll be glad you're wearing the **Van Helsing Slayer Supplies and Equipment Company's** ever-popular Rubber Briefs (guaranteed leakproof).

If you encounter a pack, you should either find a way to slay them one by one, or collect your equipment and tiptoe away. For anyone ~~stupid~~ brave enough to face them all at once, my advice is this:

1 Every pack has a leader, known as the **alpha** werewolf. This will usually be the **biggest** and strongest. Slaying this werewolf might make the others think twice before tangling with you. Or it might not - you will soon find out. One good shot, and the rest may turn tail and flee. That, or you will be almost instantly buried beneath a pile of snarling, hungry hell beasts. Good luck with that.

2 Run. Run as fast as you can. **Do not stop.** Do not turn around. **Scream** if you want to. It won't make any difference, but it might make you feel a little better for two or three seconds until the pack runs you down.

Chapter 6

How to Slay a Werewolf

And so we come to the most **important** part of your journey: slaying. I hope you have learned your lessons well, young slayer. You will need everything I have taught you, plus nerves of steel and sturdy pants. Remember: there is nothing to fear except fear itself (and a dirty great brute with teeth that could snap a lamppost in two). As the werewolf comes at you through the dark, its eyes glowing and its filthy breath shriveling your eyebrows, stay calm, stop your knees from knocking, and give it a wink. **YOU** are a slayer, and a slayer tweaks the nose of fear and laughs in the face of death.

You will need one other thing - something that no book can teach: sharp wits. Successful slayers always stay one step ahead of their prey. Perhaps the best way to demonstrate is with one of my own cases:

VAN HELSING VERSUS THE BEAST OF WRIGGLESWORTH MOOR.

It started with a **letter**...

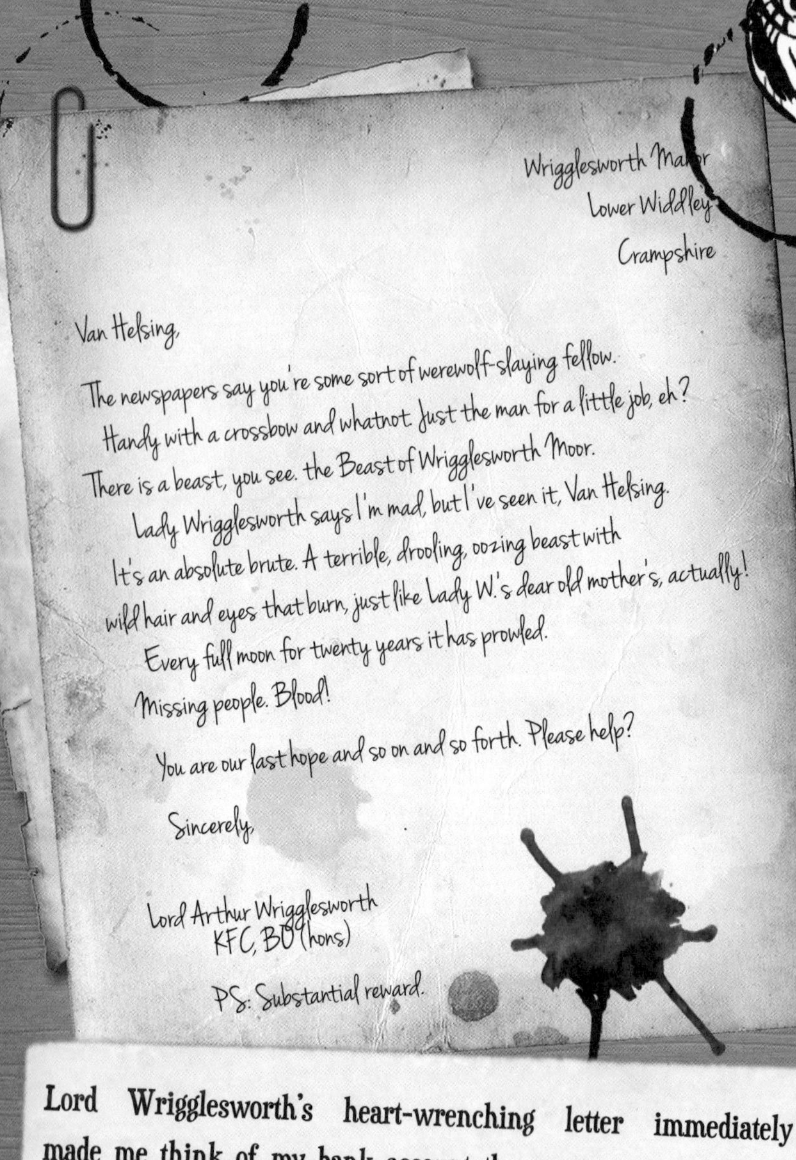

Wrigglesworth Manor
Lower Widdley
Crampshire

Van Helsing,

The newspapers say you're some sort of werewolf-slaying fellow.
Handy with a crossbow and whatnot. Just the man for a little job, eh?
There is a beast, you see. the Beast of Wrigglesworth Moor.
Lady Wrigglesworth says I'm mad, but I've seen it, Van Helsing.
It's an absolute brute. A terrible, drooling, oozing beast with
wild hair and eyes that burn, just like Lady W.'s dear old mother's, actually!
Every full moon for twenty years it has prowled.
Missing people. Blood!

You are our last hope and so on and so forth. Please help?

Sincerely,

Lord Arthur Wrigglesworth
KFC, BO (hons)

PS: Substantial reward.

Lord Wrigglesworth's heart-wrenching letter immediately made me think of ~~my bank account~~ the poor, terrorized people of Lower Widdley. Only the great Van Helsing could release them from their nightmare. Quickly, I dashed off a reply to Lord Wrigglesworth in my own top-secret, unbreakable code.

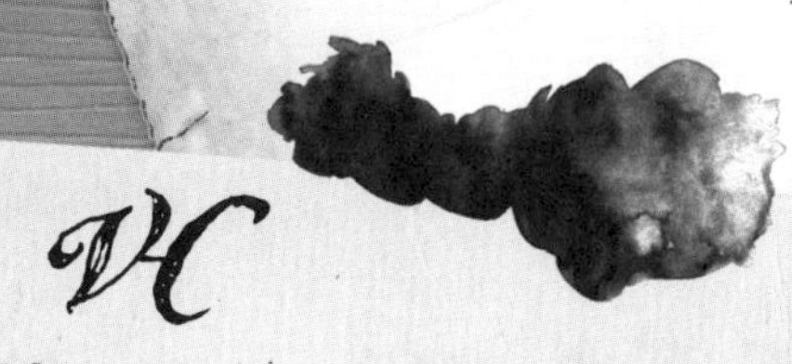

My dear Lord Wrigglesworth,

I am cabbage. Spank no one. Seaweed is of the utmost irrelevance.
I will confuse you when my invertibrations are ham.

Love,

Van

I checked the calendar. The next full moon was the following night. Quickly, I packed weapons, traps, and slaying clothes. Disguised as Jeremy Poot, an inspector of drains, I caught the train to Crampshire that very afternoon.

The train arrived at sunset. At first sight, Lower Widdley seemed to be a nice little village of thatched cottages and cheese shops. But I found there was no jewelry shop (no **silver!**), and every house had iron bars on the windows. It reminded me of Grüselighausen. An old inn – the Dog and Crumpet – stood on a wide green. I entered, already alert for signs of werewolves.

Inside, the inn was dark, lit only by a few dripping candles. Behind the bar, a grizzled-looking fellow with pointed ears, hairy knuckles, and eyebrows that met in the middle was scratching his head. "**Excuse me, sir,**" he said. "Touch of the fleas."

A-ha! I thought to myself. *I shall need to keep a close eye on this fellow...*

"Top of the evening to you, my good man," I said aloud. "Do you have a room available? I am Jeremy Poot, Her Majesty's Inspector of Drains. I shall be staying in your charming village for a few days while I inspect the... aaah... drains." Quietly, I added, "Woof woof," just to see what he would make of it.

"If you don't mind, sir, I'm a happily married man," he replied with a sniff. "Room three is available." Turning, he cried out, "Mrs. *Buuuuuurbage.*"

A hunched old woman appeared. Hair sprouted from her ears. She snuffled as she walked towards me, and I leaned back – the stench of her breath could have peeled the paint from the walls.

"My wife, the lovely **Mrs. Burbage**," the innkeeper explained. "She'll take your bags."

I stared, aghast, as Mrs. Burbage shuffled away. Could I have found not one but *two* werewolves so quickly?

Shaken, I ordered a pint of the local ale - **Vicar's Armpit**, I think it was called - and looked around the inn.

My jaw dropped open.

Sitting at a table was a woman with a big beard talking to a man so hairy that only his eyes could be seen through the thick mat of fur on his head. A man with sharp, yellow fingernails tore at a raw steak with his teeth. Everywhere I looked, there were hair and ears and twitching noses and enormous eyebrows. My gaze rested on a petite, red-haired woman with the smoothest, softest skin I had ever seen. "**Who** is that?" I asked the innkeeper.

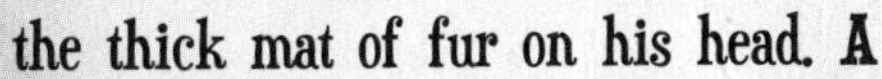

"**Miss Larkin**, the social studies teacher. A *strange* woman."

I shook my head. What kind of topsy-turvy village was **Lower Widdley**, where only the social studies teacher - usually the hairiest of people - looked normal? Were the villagers one huge pack of werewolves? My slayer senses told me to run, but I kept cool. "Mr. Burbage," I said. "May I pay with these **silver coins?**"

He grabbed them from my hand with a "Thank you kindly, sir" and bit one to make sure it was real.

Once again, my jaw dropped. A werewolf would rather put a wasps' nest in its mouth than silver. Clearly, it was going to be tricky to find the werewolf of Lower Widdley. From what I had already seen, it could be any one of several dozen people. "Do you have a local newspaper?" I asked, thinking I might find some clues there.

I took a slurp of Vicar's Armpit as I read. But there was no sign of the mysterious disappearances Lord Wrigglesworth had told me about. The front page of the *Lower Widdley Gazette* told me that Mr. Crowther of Dump Street had been attacked by ducks while fishing in the local pond, and Mrs. Gertrude Ulcer had won the Annual Toad Bake for the third year in a row. I tossed it away.

"Hey!" said a voice from the darkness at the back of the pub. "You ain't no drains inspector. You're that bloke from the papers. That nutty Professor Van Helspring – the slayer."

Silence fell like a very quiet hammer. A sea of hairy faces scowled at me.

Drat, I thought to myself. *So much for disguises.* I decided I would have to be honest. "Yes, you're right," I declared, throwing aside my wig and glasses. "Jeremy Poot was just a disguise. In fact, I am the great Professor Van Helsing, come to rid you of the werewolf curse."

"**Shhh!** We don't talk of such things, Mr. Poot," hissed Burbage, who seemed a little slow to catch on. "It's **dangerous.**"

"More than our lives are worth, talking to the likes of him," said Mrs. Burbage.

"And there's no point talking, anyway," said Burbage. "It's a full moon tomorrow. If you've come a-hunting the beast-that-is-not-named, Mr. Poot, you'll be dead by midnight. Enjoy the taste of the Vicar's Armpit while you still can!"

I went to bed with a sick feeling in my stomach, and not just from the ale. The next day was no better - my enquiries were just as fruitless as the night before. News of my mission had spread. No one would speak to me. Most of the villagers scuttled away when they saw me coming. There was only one way I was going to find this beast.

I would have to track it.

As the sun disappeared below the horizon through the barred window of dingy room three, I slipped into my third-best slayer outfit: thick, silver-stitched underwear, a suit of midnight black with a heavy leather coat, silver rings, and a wide-brimmed hat. I added a woolly scarf and tucked some mittens into my pocket. It looked like it would be a chilly night. When tracking, speed is essential, and so I picked my weapons with care: a large crossbow that I slung over my back, a sword, caltrops, four knives and three daggers, two silver-bullet pistols, and a set of Transylvanian Wolf Clamps. Plus, of course, an Exploding Chicken. I added a pair of night-vision binoculars and my Detect-o-Wolf hearing apparatus. And a ham sandwich.

I was ready.

As I left the inn, with a nod to the silent customers, village doors and shutters banged shut around me. A full moon was already climbing into the sky. All I had to do was find the werewolf and slay it. Or, I could catch the train home and put my feet up by the fire. The 10:17 p.m. to London was due at any moment.

It was tempting, but a **Van Helsing** (almost) *never* runs away from a werewolf. Not until it's absolutely necessary, at least (or sometimes because I suddenly remember I have an urgent appointment at the hair salon). **Shaking** my head, I vaulted over a fence and rolled around in muck to disguise my smell. I smiled as I rubbed cow dung into my face.

Once again, **Van Helsing** was on the hunt.

The moon shone down as I ran across the moor. Keeping to the shadows, I stopped here and there, listening through the **Van Helsing Detect-o-Wolf** and scanning the horizon with my binoculars.

Nothing.

The werewolf was out there though. It *had* to be.

At exactly midnight, an unmistakable howl drifted across the moor: Arr-oooooooooo. Quickly, I made my way towards the sound and soon picked up the werewolf's prints - it looked to be a *huge* beast. Its head would make a marvelous footstool for my den.

Arr-oooooooooooooooooooooooo.

The **howl** was louder now. I noticed a sign for **Creaking Bottom** Farm. So that was where the **beast** was heading!

I arrived just in time. A massive werewolf stood hunched in the farmyard, its teeth around the ankle of a young man. He **screamed** as the beast dragged him across the ground.

I took my crossbow and silently slipped a bolt in. A light breeze caught my coat, flapping it open as I stood **silhouetted** against the full moon. If my face hadn't been smeared with cow dung, I would have looked *extremely* nifty. Still, there was nothing I could do about that. No one ever said being a slayer is easy.

I clicked the safety catch off the crossbow. The werewolf's ears **pricked** up instantly. Dropping the young farmer, who curled up on the ground, it turned to face me. A snarl appeared on its hideous face, its teeth dripping in the moonlight. **Bloodshot eyes** glared at me through matted, greasy fur.

"**Hello, pretty,**" I said, quietly. "I *love* what you've done with your hair."

For a second, the beast looked shocked. It had probably never before seen a human who wasn't screaming.

The look passed in a moment. Roaring in fury, the werewolf sprang at me.

I fired the **crossbow**.

The beast dodged. It was fast – too fast. I gulped. There was no time for traps and gizmos. I had to think quickly...

But the werewolf was already upon me, its foul breath in my face as it knocked me to the ground. A mountain of stinking fur and muscle held me pinned on the cold stone.

It snarled. Its jaws opened.

Drool dripped.

It was all quite awful.

I was certain I was dead.

Then I heard a shout:

"Get off him, you **wacky weirdo!"**

A heavy boot landed on the side of the beast's head, and a flaming torch was thrust in its face. The farmer! The werewolf reared back, freeing one of my arms. I punched it on the nose with a fistful of silver rings and sprang to my feet as it howled in pain and scrabbled backwards.

Drawing my sword, I said, "This is a **Van Helsing Slayer Supplies and Equipment Company Number Three Broadsword – the WolfSlicer.** It is razor sharp and plated with silver. Also, I have an Exploding Chicken in my pocket."

The werewolf looked from me to the farmer and back again. It snarled again, baring its **razor-sharp teeth**. Then it stopped, lifted its hairy ears, and bounded away. In a second, it was gone.

Looking down, I saw that the werewolf's claws had shredded my third-best pants. I scowled. The great Van Helsing would have his revenge. In the meantime, I took a map from my pocket and studied the direction in which the werewolf had fled.

"You're that **mad professor** who everyone's whispering about," interrupted the farmer. "You saved my life. How can I ever repay you?"

I handed him my card.

"I don't have anything to reward you with, professor, sir," said the farmer. "Unless you likes turnips. I've got lots of turnips."

"Keep your turnips," I said, looking up from the map. "Perhaps, instead, you could do me a **favor**..."

"So, the beast got away, did it?" mumbled Lord Wrigglesworth the next afternoon. "Pity."

We were standing in the entrance hall of Wrigglesworth Manor, a fine old house of turrets and red brick. His lordship was a tall, gray fellow with a drooping mustache, a drooping nose, and drooping eyes. "This time it escaped me, my lord," I admitted. "But there is another **full moon** this evening. Tonight it won't be so lucky, not with the trap I have planned."

"Good man, Van Helsing. Where?"

I looked around the entrance hall. It had a main door of thick oak and iron. The windows were too small for any werewolf but would provide excellent escape routes for a medium-sized slayer. Perfect. "Here, if you please, my lord. And I will need **bait**."

"**Meat?**" asked Lord Wrigglesworth.

"A screaming young woman is *traditional,* my lord."

At that moment, **Lady Wrigglesworth** reappeared. A tall woman with a face like a pickaxe, she had been staring at me with disgust all morning. She cleared her throat and looked over the top of her spectacles. "You may use our daughter," she said.

Lord Wrigglesworth started. "*Lucy?*" he gurgled. "My own, sweet *Lucy*? Are you sure, my dear?"

"Since I don't believe a word of this silly werewolf nonsense, what is the worst that could happen?" Lady W. sniffed.

"Well, she could be eaten," muttered Lord Wrigglesworth.

"**Stuff** and **nonsense**," sneered Lady W. "Even if werewolves do exist, I'm sure Lucy will be perfectly safe with the professor."

For the remainder of the day, I prepared the manor. I spread **silver caltrops** around the main entrance and fitted the doors with springs to prevent the werewolf from escaping. Tripwires lay across the floor.

"My daughter, Lucy," said Lord Wrigglesworth, as I finished laying my traps. I turned around – on his arm was a young woman with curly blonde hair. "You *will* take care of her, won't you, Van Helsing, right?"

"Oh yes, my lord," I told him, raising an eyebrow. "You can be certain of that."

Turning to Lucy, I explained her part in the plan. She would scream to attract the werewolf's attention, and the beast would bound through the doors and make straight for her, setting off every trap, while I fired from the top of the stairs with a crossbow and pistols. "It will be dead before it's halfway across the room," I said confidently.

"How exciting," giggled Lucy, clapping her hands together.

"Too exciting for me, I'm sure," Lady W. interrupted with a sniff of contempt. "I shall have an early night. One of my headaches is coming on."

Together, Lord Wrigglesworth and I enjoyed a dinner of roast pheasant and a pint of Grandad's Bathwater. Then he retired to the shed to watch through a pair of binoculars.

All was ready. It was time to slay a werewolf.

Slowly, a full moon rose over Wrigglesworth Manor. I took my position at the top of the stairs – well out of harm's way – and nodded towards Lucy. She filled her lungs and let out an ear-splitting shriek. "Excellent," I told her. "And again if you please, young lady."

It wasn't long before I heard an Arr-ooooooooo from across the moor. The wolf was soon at the door – its great shadow fell across the hallway. A second later, it crept into Wrigglesworth Manor, snarling.

BOOM. The door slammed shut behind it, shaking the manor's ancient stones.

"Oh my, what big teeth you have," screamed Lucy, clasping her hands together in girlish fear.

The werewolf bounded across the hall, setting off my traps. Metal jaws clanged shut and crossbow bolts zipped and zinged across the room, breaking a number of valuable vases that I had forgotten to remove.

But something was wrong. The werewolf had neatly avoided every trap. And it wasn't pouncing at the beautiful and very appetizing Lucy. It was bounding towards. . .

ME!

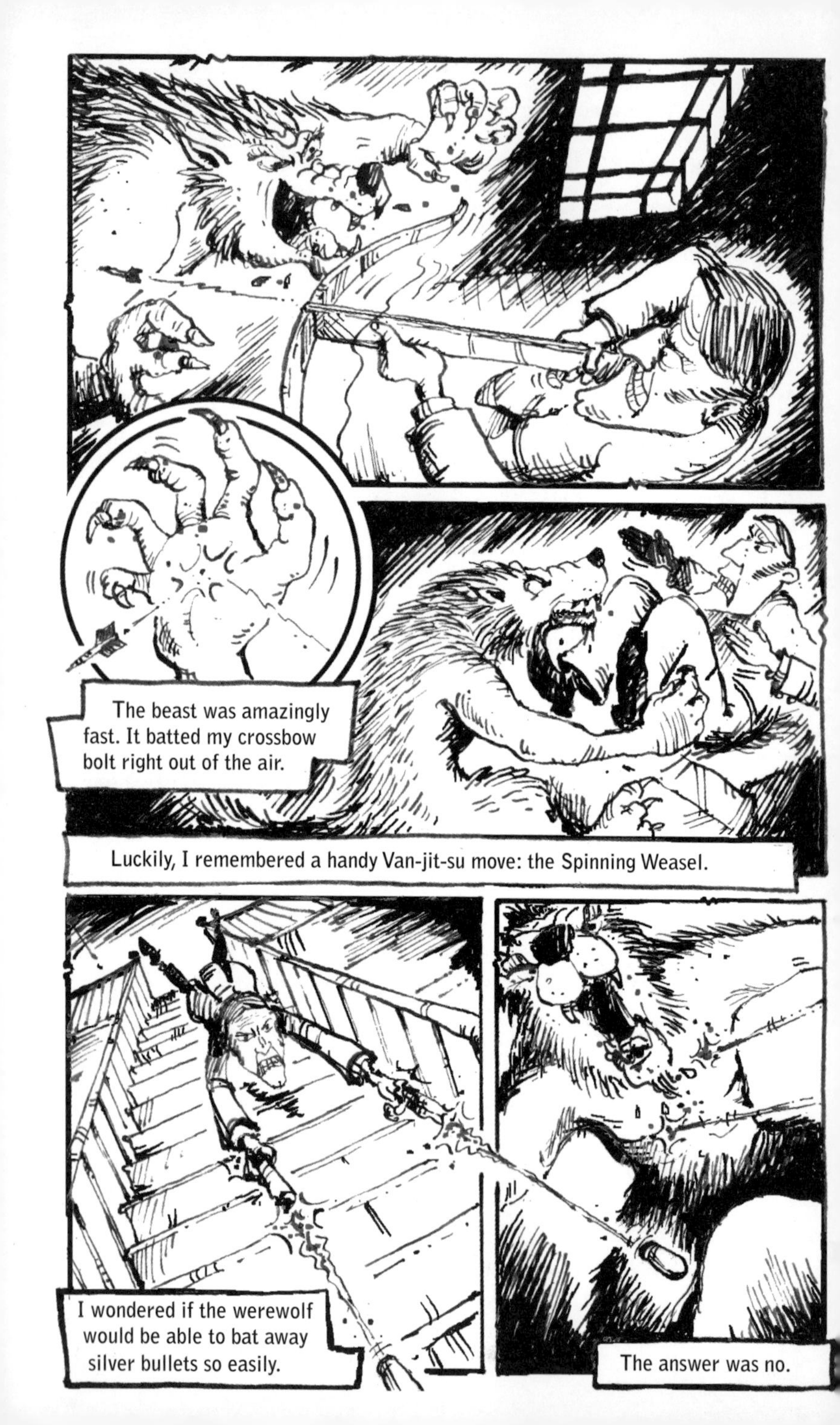
The beast was amazingly fast. It batted my crossbow bolt right out of the air.
Luckily, I remembered a handy Van-jit-su move: the Spinning Weasel.
I wondered if the werewolf would be able to bat away silver bullets so easily.
The answer was no.

Unfortunately, it still had some fight left in it.
I had no choice but to use the ultimate Van-jit-su move...
...the Screaming Eagle Falling from the Sky with Two Silver Daggers!
From behind me I heard a low, evil growl. I froze.
Drop your weapons and get away from my MOTHER.
Your mother?! Lady Wrigglesworth?

Yes, meddling slayer.
You thought that you had prepared a trap for the werewolf, but instead you walked right into ours. Now, I'm hungry. I think we'll start with your legs, as they look quite yummy.

I remembered my own advice: **NEVER** take on more than one werewolf at a time. Things were looking bad.

Or were they?
Ladies, before you eat me, there are three things you should know. First, I guessed last night that there was a werewolf at Wrigglesworth Manor when I followed the beast's direction on the map.

Second, in his letter, Lord Wrigglesworth told me that the beast reminded him of Lady W.'s mother. And, Lucy, you're a pretty girl but your breath stinks like an old man's underwear. It's these little things a slayer notices.

Third, a good slayer always has a final surprise.

Oh, and fourth, a good slayer knows when to RUN.

The farmer had done his job well. The villagers of Lower Widdley wouldn't trust a stranger but they would trust him – one of their own. Lady Wrigglesworth and her daughter would never escape the fire started by the villagers' torches.
So, your little werewolf problem has been solved, Lord Wrigglesworth. Is it a bad time to talk about that reward?
And that, young slayer, is how to slay a werewolf.

Professor
Van Helsing Phd BA Dip GNVQ
BSC PGCE
HND
BE
BEC CBic
BDA
BSM
CD
CGEO

Chapter 7
Last Words

"Professor Van Helsing," I hear you say. "You are an amazing teacher. Totally awesome."

I know, young slayer, but hold on just one moment. If you have learned your lessons well and trained hard, the very sight of you will strike fear into the ghastly, ravenous heart of every werewolf. Nevertheless, while every slayer needs a confident swagger (as well as the ability to flick boogers in the face of certain death), a slayer who is *too* confident is a slayer who is destined to find out what a werewolf looks like from the inside. Before you steal out into the night, as quiet as a shadow, as deadly as a year-old ham sandwich, there are still a few things you should know...

The Checklist

An essential part of your preparations, the checklist should be completed before every slaying. Even a first-class brain like mine sometimes forgets **important details**, and the last thing you want to be doing as a werewolf leaps at you with moonlight glinting off its dripping fangs is rummaging around for that pistol you're *sure* you packed. Make a list and check off *everything* before attempting to slay. It should look something like this. . .

CHECKLIST

☐ Are all my gizmos packed and my weapons sharp, ready to use, and in the right pockets? [16]

☐ Have I abstained from beans and cabbage for at least twenty-four hours? Silence is often key to survival - do not be betrayed by your own behind.

☐ Is my hair styled and my outfit looking snazzy? A slayer without style is just a slob with a crossbow.

☐ Do I have a plan and back-up plans? You will have to think on your feet, but do **NOT** try making up plans as you go. Slayers often lose concentration when a werewolf is trying to rip their ears off.

☐ Are all my traps laid and tested? (Be careful with this - slaying is *much* more difficult if you are hanging upside down by one ankle in your own trap.)

☐ Is the moon full? It is surprising how many slayers forget to check. Spending all night squatting in a bush or twiddling your thumbs in a carefully prepared trap is both dull and embarrassing.

[16] I once tried to pull a dagger from my pocket only to find that I had packed a cheese sandwich by mistake. Luckily, the cheese was extremely sharp.

When Slaying Goes Wrong

Had an off day? Slaying not gone quite to plan? If so, you'll probably be dead by now (in which case you need not read the rest of this section). However, you may just be lucky and only lose an arm or a leg or two. Don't be downhearted - every slayer collects a few scars along the way and they make for great stories to share with other slayers. Check out my own on the right...

If things do go wrong, the most important advice to remember is: **DON'T PANIC!** Keep a cool head (even if it's in a werewolf's mouth) and you might still make it out alive. If you have a weapon within reach, then what are you waiting for? Either get on with it or sprinkle some salt and pepper on yourself. If not, you can try poking the beast in the eye or biting it on the nose, but a werewolf drooling over its next meal is not easy to distract. At times like these, you need **Van Helsing's Last Resort.**

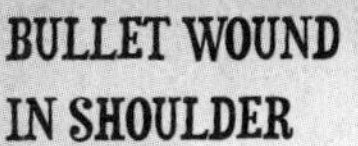

BULLET WOUND IN SHOULDER

This is where a screaming young lady shot me by mistake while I was wrestling a werewolf. (Note: Never give your bait weapons unless they have had their eyesight fully checked.)

MISSING EARLOBE

I lost my earlobe to a Kitsune during a struggle in a Chinese restaurant. The cheeky devil dipped it in soy sauce and swallowed it whole.

CLAW MARKS DOWN CHEST

I collected this scar during some rough-and-tumble with a Mexican Nagual that surprised me in the bath. I eventually choked it to death by shoving a rubber duck down its throat.

LARGE SCAR DOWN ARM

This scar was given to me by Herman Schnausermann all those years ago in Grüselighausen. It reminds me never to underestimate the evil of werewolves, or bank managers.

LARGE BITE MARK ON LEG

This beauty was given to me by a werewolf in Sweden. The beast wasn't quite as dead as I thought it was as I tested it out as a new fireside rug.

Next Steps for the Successful Slayer

Don't fear, dear reader - after following the steps in this book, it is highly likely you will be **victorious**. The werewolf will lie dead at your feet and, thanks to you, the world is a safer place. **Hurrah** for you (and for me, because I trained you). **But** what next? **A** nice, hot bubble bath before collecting your reward and facing the cheering crowd? No, young slayer - your job is not yet finished. You can't just leave a dead werewolf lying around the place.

"Hold on there, Van," **you say.** "I've done all the hard work, can't someone else bury the revolting thing?"

But wait: don't bury it. That would be a waste. **A** *live* werewolf is an ugly brute but a *dead* werewolf can be both attractive and useful. **And** after trying to tear you limb from limb, the least the beast can do is help decorate your home. Werewolf skin makes luxurious rugs and cushions, and the fur can also provide delightfully warm hats, coats, and gloves, but use your imagination - almost every part of a werewolf can be used (be sure to wash it thoroughly in hot, soapy water first). **Here** are just a few ideas...

The Coat Rack

A stuffed werewolf by the front door makes an excellent place to hang your coat and is sure to impress your guests.

The Remote-Control Werewolf Butler

Slayers who like pottering around in the gadget laboratory may wish to use a few gizmos to create their own wolfy butler. Not only will your guests be thrilled when served tea by a "real" werewolf, but the remote-control werewolf butler is guaranteed to get rid of door-to-door salesmen, rent collectors, and anyone else you'd rather not speak to.

The Mounted Head

A design classic, the mounted werewolf head makes an excellent souvenir of your hunt and adds a note of elegance to any room (except the bathroom - the sudden sight of a snarling werewolf head can lead to guests to having little "accidents").

Key Hook

Tired of losing your keys? That's not likely to happen again if your key holder is made from a handsome, stuffed werewolf paw. These can also be used as toast or letter racks, combs, salad tongs, and even attractive hair clips.

Back Scrubber

The werewolf's tail is long and bristly - perfect for cleaning those hard-to-reach places at bath time!

Bookmark

Even a werewolf's ear can be useful! And every time you open your current bedtime reading (I recommend *Why I Am Fabulous*, by Prof. V. Helsing), you'll be reminded of your glorious victory.

Farewell, and Happy Slaying

Congratulations, young slayer, you are ready to prowl the night in search of your first werewolf. Be warned: there will be people who call you mad. They will laugh and jeer and poke fun at you. Ignore them (or give them a swift kick in the buttocks if you prefer). It doesn't matter. We know better. *We* know that the rewards of exterminating these diabolical vermin are enormous.

Firstly, you will have all the fur underwear anyone could dream of. Secondly, beast by drooling beast we are pushing back the dark tide of Evil and all that. Thirdly, and most importantly, there are the *actual* rewards - the standard rate is **$10,000** per werewolf, plus expenses.[17]

Farewell for now, young slayer. Wherever you hunt, I wish you many moonlight adventures and leave you with one last piece of advice: if at first you don't succeed, then you'll be eaten, in which case slaying is probably not for you. Still, you can rest assured that if you *do* become a werewolf's dinner, Professor Van Helsing will give you a full refund for the price of this book. All you have to do is apply in person.

Happy slaying.

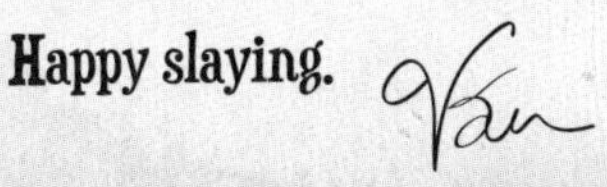

[17] People will try to talk the price down. I show my scars and tell them that if they don't want to pay the full reward, they can always slay the werewolf themselves. It's amazing how quickly they get their wallets out.

INTRODUCING THE VAN HELSING'S SECRET MINIBOW

SPECIALLY DESIGNED FOR THOSE "UP-CLOSE AND PERSONAL" MOMENTS, THE VAN HELSING'S SECRET DELIVERS A SURPRISE NO WEREWOLF WILL BE EXPECTING: A PERFECTLY FORMED MINIBOLT OF PUREST SILVER.

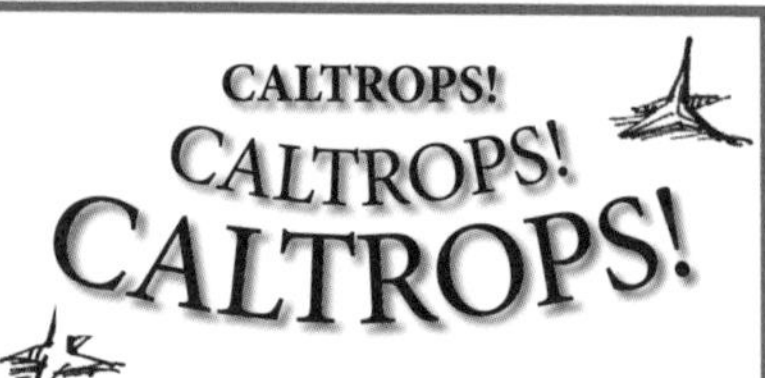

"Easily hidden inside your sleeve, the Van Helsing's Secret fits any wrist. And you'll LOVE my new QuikFlik wrist-action firing technology."

Van

only $39.99

CALTROPS! CALTROPS! CALTROPS!

THE SLAYER'S BEST FRIEND!

SOLID SILVER

Watch that WEREWOLF dance!

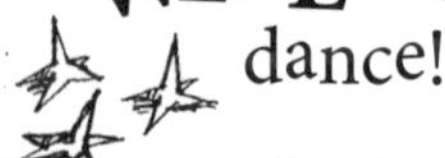

$49.99 for a bag of six

For a punch that packs a whole lot of pain!

SILVER KNUCKLEDUSTERS:

Choose from **TEN** designs, from **"Spiked Fist of Fury"** to **"Snarling Werewolf Head"**

Makes a perfect gift - ask us to engrave your knuckleduster with a message of love.

$69.99

Fall Sword Sale

We have everything from secret swordsticks for city slayers to double-handled broadswords for those "screaming berserker" moments, all at giveaway prices!

BUY ONE OF OUR AWARD-WINNING WOLF-BE-GONE LONGSWORDS AND GET A MATCHING SET OF STEAK KNIVES!